PENGUIN METRO READS

YOU WERE MY CRUSH . . .

DURJOY DATTA was born and brought up in New Delhi. He completed a degree in engineering and business management before embarking on a writing career. His first book, *Of Course I Love You . . .*, was published when he was twenty-one years old and was an instant bestseller. His successive novels—*Now That You're Rich . . .*, *She Broke Up, I Didn't!*, *Oh Yes, I Am Single!*, *If It's Not Forever . . .*, *Someone Like You*—have also found prominence on various bestseller lists, making him one of the highest-selling authors in India. Durjoy lives in New Delhi, loves dogs and is an active CrossFitter.

For more updates, you can follow him on Facebook (www.facebook.com/durjoydatta1) or Twitter (@durjoydatta).

ORVANA GHAI was born in New Delhi. She is a postgraduate in marketing from University of Westminster, London. She has worked with international fashion labels, event management companies and NGOs in the past. She loves to dance and holds diplomas in various dance forms. This is her first book.

To know more about her follow her on Facebook.

Also by Durjoy Datta

Hold My Hand

*

She Broke Up, I Didn't!
I Just Kissed Someone Else!

*

Till the Last Breath ...

*

Of Course I Love You
Till I Find Someone Better
(With Maanvi Ahuja)

*

Oh Yes, I'm Single!
And So Is My Girlfriend!
(With Neeti Rustagi)

*

Now That You're Rich
Let's Fall in Love!
(With Maanvi Ahuja)

*

Someone Like You
(With Nikita Singh)

*

If It's Not Forever
It's Not Love
(With Nikita Singh)

You Were My Crush

Till You Said You Love Me!

DURJOY
DATTA

ORVANA
GHAI

Penguin
metro reads

PENGUIN BOOKS

Published by the Penguin Group

Penguin Books India Pvt. Ltd, 7th Floor, Infinity Tower C, DLF Cyber City, Gurgaon 122 002, Haryana, India

Penguin Group (USA) Inc., 375 Hudson Street, New York, New York 10014, USA

Penguin Group (Canada), 90 Eglinton Avenue East, Suite 700, Toronto, Ontario, M4P 2Y3, Canada

Penguin Books Ltd, 80 Strand, London WC2R 0RL, England

Penguin Ireland, 25 St Stephen's Green, Dublin 2, Ireland (a division of Penguin Books Ltd)

Penguin Group (Australia), 707 Collins Street, Melbourne, Victoria 3008, Australia

Penguin Group (NZ), 67 Apollo Drive, Rosedale, Auckland 0632, New Zealand

Penguin Books (South Africa) (Pty) Ltd, Block D, Rosebank Office Park, 181 Jan Smuts Avenue, Parktown North, Johannesburg 2193, South Africa

Penguin Books Ltd, Registered Offices: 80 Strand, London WC2R 0RL, England

First published by Grapevine India Publishers Pvt. Ltd 2011
Published in Penguin Metro Reads by Penguin Books India 2013

ISBN 9780143421559

Typeset in Adobe Caslon Pro by Eleven Arts, Delhi
Printed at Replika Press Pvt. Ltd, India

A PENGUIN RANDOM HOUSE COMPANY

To the coolest brother anyone could ever have.
Benoy, this is for you!

Chapter One

Ever seen the guy who drives like a maniac in a ridiculously big car? The guy with the powerful dad? The big house? Well, I am *that* guy.

Benoy Roy.

I am not flashy, but I have a big car and a big house, and there is no hiding that. But yes, I do not look rich. I stand five feet and ten inches tall and look like someone you would miss on a busy road. Wheatish complexion, slim, with short, neat hair—that is what my matrimonial ad would read like. Often, I have heard people say, *He does not look that rich.* I do not blame them; I was never impressed by what I saw in the mirror either.

Well, it was another morning for me. I was in no hurry again. Life was awesome. I did not have to worry about the early morning lecture, shouting professors or pending assignments.

My head did not hurt even though I was sure I had got

sloshed the night before, since I was on the couch and not on my bed where I should have been! I was still in the clothes I had worn the previous night to the club.

I must have passed out, I thought.

These nights of excessive drinking, blackouts and bad hangovers were becoming a routine. *This is the last time I am drinking*, I said to myself. I was lying. I tried to remember why I had not gone up to my bedroom and slept, but I really could not. I tried to recall the girl I had danced with the previous night, but I could not remember that clearly either. I remembered the name though. *Palak*. I smiled. She was pretty, and Deb had introduced me to her.

As I heated the coffee and poured it into a cup, my phone rang. It was Eshaan and he asked me the same question that he did every day. *Was I going to college that day?* No, I was not! I didn't have a hangover but I did not want to spoil that day sitting on those broken benches, beneath the creaky fans. Moreover, three back-to-back lectures were not my thing! Just as I switched on the television, the door was flung wide open. It was the maid. I looked at her, and she smiled. She had the newspaper in her hand; she kept it on the table. Though the house was *pretty* big, I lived alone and so never had much work for her to do.

'Benoy? What *is* in the sink?' she asked, disgusted.

'What?' I asked as I entered the kitchen.

'Come and see for yourself.' She had covered her face with her pallu.

I walked up to the sink and a pungent smell hit my nose. I looked at it and it almost made me puke. It was filthy and it smelled worse than a dead rat.

'*Damn it.*'

'Babu, you drank too much last night?' she said in a muffled tone from behind the pallu.

'I guess so.'

I asked her to go and shop for vegetables; I told her I would take care of it by the time she came back. She grabbed the shopping bag and left the house as soon as possible. I stood there for a while, disgusted at what I had done. This was new. I used to black out, but I *never* used to puke. The drainpipe was blocked and I thought, *Why don't they just make bigger drainpipes?*

Because people are meant to puke in toilets, dumbass, a voice in my head said.

I did not waste any more time. I wrapped a handkerchief around my face and got to work with a plunger and that day's newspaper in my hand. Fifteen *stinking* minutes later, the sink sparkled and I stank.

I am never drinking again! Definitely! I said to myself as I entered the shower.

I loved the shower area. It was the second-best place after the gym I had set up a couple of months back. It cost me . . . well, I do not know *how* much, for my father paid for it. All I know is that I loved it. Meanwhile, the maid was back and she had started to cook.

'*Aunty!* A little less oil,' I shouted out as I came down the stairs.

'Babu, where will you get the strength? And stop drinking so much, babu. It's not good for you,' she shouted back.

Just as I flopped on the couch, the doorbell rang.

'Who's it?' I shouted from where I was sitting. The door was being banged now. *Harder*.

'*FINE!*'

'Deb?' I exclaimed. Debashish was my cousin, five years older than me. He had turned twenty-five just the day before, and it was his party last night. LAST. DRINKING. NIGHT. EVER.

'Fuck you, Benoy,' he said, and he looked pissed. 'Where have you been? I have been calling you for the last twenty minutes. Anyway, where is Palak?'

'Palak?'

'Benoy? I don't have time for this. Her mom has been calling me since the morning; she's freaking out. Where *is* she?'

'I don't know what you're talking about, Deb!'

'What? You left with her last night. Don't you fucking *remember*?'

He started looking everywhere and I followed him around; he was clearly freaking out and was out of his goddamn mind.

'No! I do not,' I insisted.

'Did you guys come home? You said you would drop her at her friend's place?'

Deb's phone was ringing constantly.

'I don't remember, Deb. All I remember is that we were there in the club and you guys were there too, and then I woke up on this couch. That's it!'

'You were on the couch? Then where the hell is she?' he demanded and sprinted up the stairs. I still had no clue as to what was happening.

'PALAK?' he shouted and entered the bedroom.

As I followed him into my bedroom, and tried to remember the sequence of events from the previous night, I saw him bent over an unconscious girl who lay on the side of my bed. Palak! We both helped her sit up on the bed. She was still falling all over us and she stank of beer.

'Huh?' Palak looked up, still not in her senses.

'PALAK. Wake up!' Deb said. 'Your mom called me up. She wants to know where you are. *Where* is your phone?' Deb kept repeating these sentences.

'Benoy? Don't just stand there. Get her some water!'

'Fine,' I said and sprinted downstairs.

As I came back upstairs, I saw Palak mumble something. I was in a state of mild shock! I really had not expected *this*, even from myself. I had no memory of getting a girl home. It was not really the first time though, but usually I remember.

'Where is my phone? What did Mom say? Is she angry? Does *he* know? Did *he* call?' she asked a million questions. I tried to avoid her gaze as I looked for a room freshener. She *stank*.

She was freaking out, and she held her head. I stood there wondering whether it was in regret or if it was the hangover. I wanted to ask her, but I thought it would be better to let Deb handle it. He had been in a relationship for over five years now. He had more experience in handling crying females than me.

'Relax, Palak, don't cry. I told your mom that you were with Avantika. And that you're fine. You really don't remember where your phone is?' he asked her.

She shook her head and tears streamed down her cheeks in full flow. *Thank God for Deb!*

'Okay, just go wash your face and then I will drop you home,' Deb said to her and she left.

'Benoy? Are you CRAZY?' Deb almost shouted.

'What, Dada? She is your friend not mine. I can't help it if *she* is crazy.'

'She is not supposed to be here. *You* got her here. You are the one who is crazy, not her. And what would I say to Avantika? You have screwed me, man!'

'Why are you so afraid of Avantika?' I asked.

'I am not. I just like *not* to screw up things with her,' Deb said.

'Whatever, I am sorry,' I said. 'Do you want me to drop her home?'

'No, I will do it. Anyway, how is your hangover? Better?' he asked, concerned. I nodded; he was my brother after all. He even *looked* like me. He was just a shade shorter than me, but he never agreed on that. We weren't the best-looking people in the world, but we had something in common—a *dimple*, a facial deformity, and it was probably the only good thing about us. Lately, we had been working out together to get ourselves a perfect set of abs, but till then, we were sexually very unappealing.

'Can we go?' Palak gulped, as she stood at the bedroom door, still crying softly.

'Sure.'

She was yet to exchange a single word with me or establish eye contact with me. Deb helped her down the stairs. Bai looked at her, surprised.

'Bye, Palak,' I said as those two were leaving through the door.

She did not say anything, just looked at me and gave me a half-hearted smile.

'I am fine,' Palak told Deb as she got inside Deb's car.

'I am going to talk to you later about this, Benoy. All this nonsense has to stop,' Deb said as he opened his car door. 'And this is the last time I am going to help you with your crushes.'

We shook hands and he said, 'And one more thing, Benoy. Go to the kitchen or somewhere. She just said she puked in your house last night. And she is sorry about it.'

Fuck! Fuck her! Fuck her! Crush? Bullshit.

Well, at least I could drink again. Later, I found her cell phone in the kitchen. I had no intention of returning it. She had *puked* in my house.

Chapter Two

The morning did not start well. I had cleaned up someone else's puke and the smell was still somewhere in my head. I had images of her puking in my sink going through my mind all morning and she was no longer cute to me! *Filthy.*

All this while, my phone kept ringing. It was Eshaan and he kept calling incessantly. I had a ground rule—*never answer Eshaan's call until he calls you for the sixth time.* If he called less than five times then it had to be something frivolous.

It had been one year in Hindu College, Delhi University, and there had not been a single day that he had not called me to let me know about the scheduled lectures, the extra classes, the extra notes that I might need, et cetera. My default state was to ignore his calls. I picked up the *sixth* call.

'Why don't you pick up my calls?' Eshaan said angrily.

'I was a little stuck,' I said. 'What happened?'

'Okay. Next time, please pick it up the first time,' he said. *Yeah, right!*

Eshaan told me that a tax-planning professor was less than impressed about being offered money (by Dad) to mark my internal exam paper (I had decided to leave the answer booklet blank) a little *leniently.* The professor wanted to talk to me in person now.

'Your father cannot buy *everything*!' Eshaan had said once.

He was not quite right. My father was a wealthy man. I was born with a silver spoon in my mouth, or diamond. You get the drift. My bank accounts were always loaded; credit-card bills were never a problem. The car I drove, the house I lived in, it was all *his* but still *mine.*

Last year, when I had screwed up my board exams and it looked like it would be hard to get into a Delhi University college, I had called up my father. Next day, I was a Delhi squash champion, and I got admission in BCom (Honours) through the sports quota. *Not bad at all, was it?* I did not hate studying, but when you have everything, education is never the top priority.

My father was kind to me but not without reason. My parents were divorced and we were never on talking terms. He was a stranger to me, and I was brought up fatherless since I was eight. I did not miss him. Until a year ago, till the time Mom was alive, he had some point of contact in the family. However, when she lost her battle to cancer last year, he had no one left. The car, the house, the gym—all these were his attempts to buy me. I was greedy enough to let him buy things, but not as much to sell *myself.*

I drove all the way to college to meet the honest, upright, asshole professor of mine. Why couldn't he just accept the money and shut up? I always assumed that professors are poorly paid. Why would he turn down *extra* money?

'Have you thought about what you will say?' Eshaan asked as soon I got down from my car.

'No. He wants to meet me, right? *He* wants to talk, not me,' I said as I walked towards the professor's offices.

'Benoy. Listen.'

Eshaan was always full of motherly advice. Nevertheless, I could not ignore Eshaan either. If there was anything I knew about BCom, it was through him. Well, not just BCom: he had my back for everything.

'Yes, Eshaan?'

'Just go in and tell him that you weren't well and you had to go home. Tell him you passed all the other exams . . . and that your dad was just concerned about your future, that's why he—'

'Eshaan? Why don't you go and talk to him?' I joked.

'I did.'

Despite the frequency, his over-involvement in my life never ceased to amaze me.

'I just asked him what the issue was and he said he would only talk to you,' he said. 'I am sorry.'

Eshaan was asking for my forgiveness because he could not *un*screw what I had screwed up. He was such a darling! Had I been a girl, I would have kissed him and hugged him. Well, maybe not.

'No, man. It's fine. I will handle it,' I said.

'If there is any problem, just call me. I will be in Kamla Nagar. Okay?'

'Sonil?' I asked him.

'Yes,' he said, as I saw him blush a little.

Relationships, I tell you, they totally fuck up even the sanest of men. He had started dating a girl from Daulat Ram College. It had been a year and he was nuts about her. Eshaan was charming, smiled more than necessary, cared more than necessary, was unnecessarily fair and was immensely likeable. He was cute, like a little brother, like a panda. It often went against him. He was often too cute for any girl.

I wished Sonil would see that, too. I *hated* her. She thought I was a vain, ill-behaved, rich brat, and an asshole. She had asked Eshaan to stay away from me, but Eshaan wasn't that stupid.

I walked through the corridors, smiling at every face that I came across. I recognized a few faces and a few of them recognized me. Last year, I had joined college with much fanfare. I drove big cars to college, argued with seniors and professors alike. Very soon, I was *in*famous in the college for my behaviour and unabashed abuse of the power I wielded. After a few days, people got busy and they promptly forgot about my existence.

Mom's condition had worsened and her chemotherapy sessions had started. I had to be with her. She had left her job and her condition deteriorated with every passing day. Doctors had not given her much time. I wanted to spend every waking second with her. She had started losing herself to cancer and it became infuriatingly tough for me. I had always seen her as a strong woman, who brought me up as a single mother—managed work and a *worthless* son. It was torturous to see her like that—frail, weak, losing weight and hair every day, vomiting and crying. Even behind those smiles she faked, I could see what she was going through.

'Benoy?' she had said.

'Yes, Maa.'

'Take care when I'm not there.' She had smiled at me.

'Don't say that,' I had said to her, with tears in my eyes. I had never imagined my life without her. 'You will be fine.'

I was lying to myself. Every single day, I saw her going through the pain. Little by little, I saw her die. I heard her in agony every day and wished I could take it away. When I used to sit on the cold, hard bench of the hospital and hear her cry, I wished that she would go peacefully rather than go through the excruciating pain every day.

I would look at the life-support equipment that kept her alive and think, *It's just making it harder for her*. It was *my mom* on the bed. She deserved better. She had done nothing to deserve this pain.

Finally, the *day* came when she left me behind. It was a very hard time for me. When my mom passed away, I stopped going to college. I had prepared myself for the loss, but nothing prepares you for death, nothing prepares you for absence. With her death, a small part of me died too. I did not cry for days. I lived in denial. I thought I would wake up some day and find her caressing my hair.

It had become impossible to live any longer in that house. The *silence* used to drive me crazy. Even months after her death, I used to go downstairs after a good night's sleep and look for her in the kitchen. I used to leave water bottles everywhere, thinking that she would be there to put them back in the fridge. I used to shout at nights, asking her for dinner only to realize that she was no longer there.

I used to remember all those times when my mother wanted to talk to me after a long day at her office and I used to be too busy on the phone with my friends. I used to regret every such moment. The uncelebrated Mother's Days. The birthdays I was not there with her. I used to feel embarrassed when Mom used to hug me in public. However, in that empty house, and in my empty life, I could have done anything to have her rest my head on her shoulder and put me to sleep. I loved my mom and I missed her every day. She left a huge void in my life. She was *everything* to me, my only family.

I underwent therapy and Deb's mom started to take care of me. Over this period, I had started to drink and smoke heavily. I did everything to fill up the emptiness in my life. Nothing worked. After the person I had loved the most *died* in my own arms, everything else stopped to matter. It took me a few months to get back to normal.

I crossed a line of staff offices with different names on them. Finally, I saw the name in bold letters—Dr S.K. Ashra (Tax Planning). I knocked on the door and the voice from the other side asked me to come in.

'Good morning, sir,' I said.

'Sit down, Benoy,' he said politely.

I was pleasantly surprised as I had expected him to blast me. That is what he had called me for, right? Eshaan had told me he had a reputation of being nasty with students. He was forty-five but looked older. With his short stature, small paunch and unintelligent looks, I would have guessed him to be a government clerk and not a professor. It was hard to believe that he had turned down a bribe. He looked like someone who would have mattresses stuffed with money from bribes.

'Thank you, sir.'

'Umm, I noticed that you did *not* give your tax exam,' he asked while sipping at his tea from the chipped teacup.

'Yes, sir.'

'Why?' he asked.

'Sir, I wasn't well,' I said, half-heartedly. I did not want to lie. I just wanted him to accept the money and get lost.

'So? You left the paper empty?' he asked.

'Yes, sir,' I said.

'You know that you can fail this subject unless you really do well in the finals,' he said, and leaned on the table.

'Yes, sir,' I said, uninterestedly. I added as an afterthought, 'Sir, what can be done?'

The conversation started to sound like I was avoiding a speeding ticket from a constable. I felt like the girl who lifts her skirt in the porn movies to get an 'A' from the old, sex-starved professor. If it was anything like that, it was going perfectly for me. Now, I just hoped he wanted money, and not me. *That* would have been weird.

'Umm,' he said, 'your father called yesterday.'

'I know,' I said. 'I am sorry about that.'

'No, no, no!' he said, his voice suddenly turned super polite. 'Your father is a *big* man! That he called me was an honour in itself.'

'Ohhh, is it?' I said. I wondered if he was being sarcastic.

I knew the *look* in his eyes. It was *greed*. It seemed he did *not* want the money. He wanted something more. After ten minutes, during which I totally lost any respect for the professor, I walked out of the room. I checked my phone and it had thirteen missed calls from Eshaan. He was tenser about the entire situation than I was. Eshaan always thought of me as a lost soul, and maybe after what happened in the first year, I *was*. Since I did not have any real friends in college, he always took it upon himself to see to it that I was not bored or feeling out of place there.

'Benoy?' he asked when I called him. 'How did it go?'

'It went well,' I said. 'I did what you asked me to. I cried a little, begged him to score me, and then he said he would give me the average marks for the exam.'

'See. I told you!' he said, genuine happiness dripping from his voice. 'Not everything can be bought!' he said again.

'Yes. You told me,' I said.

I did not tell him what really happened. After I cut the call, I did what I hated doing the most—calling up *Dad*. These calls were important and I could not run away from them. These *paid* for my life.

'Hello?' I called him up.

'Benoy? How are you?' my father said from the other side.

'Remember the tax-planning professor?' I asked.

'Yes, yes, the exam that you missed.'

'He lost your number.'

'Oh!'

'He wants more. He has kids studying abroad,' I said.

I was right. *Bedroom mattresses stuffed with money.* Eshaan was wrong. My father could buy everything.

Chapter Three

'Aunty! Not any more,' I said, as Deb's mom put another spoonful of rice on my plate. Aunty had lived her life for only two purposes.

The first was to get Deb *fat*. She had been trying to do that since forever. She had almost succeeded when Deb touched eighty-five kilograms when he was in college, but he had lost all that weight now. His mom is still fighting the depression she suffered during Deb's weight loss.

The second was to get him married to a Bengali girl in true *Bengali* style. After being the bride's mom twice, she desperately wanted to be the groom's mom once. However, Deb had crushed her dreams when he told his parents he would be marrying Avantika, a *Punjabi* girl. And since Deb wouldn't be accepted at Avantika's place, there would be no wedding. Her mom had reacted as if someone had died. She is still in shock.

'Why don't you give Deb some?' I protested. 'His plate is almost empty.'

'I don't know what he is doing,' his mom said irritably. 'He keeps saying no carbs, no oil, and spends hours in the gym. I really don't get what you youngsters try to do.'

'We try to live longer and stay fit, that's it, Maa,' he said.

'Fit? My foot! Anyway, Benoy, which coaching classes are you joining?'

'Coaching classes? For what?' I said. I really did not like where the conversation was heading.

'I mean if you decide to do management, you would have to enrol for some coaching classes right now, wouldn't you, beta?'

I don't know why she was so concerned about it. I thought it was because she wanted me to feel that I was cared for, and loved.

'It's too early. I haven't decided,' I said and stuffed my face with food so that I would not have to talk.

'Deb? Didn't you enrol in the two-year course too?' she asked and Deb nodded.

'He was dating Avantika then! He hardly studied for it. And he took three attempts to crack it,' I protested.

'Whatever,' Deb said.

'Let him do what he wants to,' said Deb's dad, who was quietly reading his newspaper up until then. I often wondered if his brother, my dad, would be like him, too.

'I made that mistake with Deb and look what he has done. He's marrying a Punjabi girl! Not even a wedding. *Chhee*,' she said, angry and dejected at the same time.

'Calm down,' Uncle said.

'I don't have a problem with Avantika but at least there should be a wedding,' she said, and it looked like she was choking on her tears.

'Calm down. They are *not* yet getting married,' Uncle said.

I could see that Deb did not like the conversation. Avantika and Deb were not seeing each other any more. However, they were still very much in love. Avantika and Deb had had a strange relationship over the years. They were the ideal couple for very many years until the time they entered college at MDI, Gurgaon, and things started to go downhill. Deb, drunk and out of his senses, cheated on Avantika, and Avantika had walked out.

After the break-up, Deb had spent months in Mumbai, without a job, trying to convince her to come back. Avantika did not budge. She had still not changed her mind despite all of Deb's efforts. Deb had never discussed his problems with Avantika with us. His eyes were stuck to the television, and it was apparent that he did not want to talk about her.

'Can we talk about something other than her?' Deb said.

'Anything other than my academic plans. Wedding plans will do! And don't worry, Aunty; I will get married to a Bengali girl. The kind of girl *you* will like,' I said.

'Sure he will,' Deb said sarcastically.

'I will,' I said and looked at Aunty.

She smiled her widest and I was happy that I had said that. It is strange how moms just care about two things in their kids' lives—*food* and *marriage*. If you do these two things correctly, it will be Mother's Day for them every day.

Soon, after that, his parents left.

'Benoy? Never bring up Avantika in front of Mom. You know how she reacts,' he said angrily.

'I am sorry,' I said. 'Anyway, did you ask Palak?'

After that incident, I had asked Deb to ask Palak if we had made out that day. Or kissed! I was just a little curious. I wanted to know if something had happened and whether I should call her and apologize. She was pretty after all and I had been single for too long.

'Nothing happened between the two of you. I had been a fool to ask you to drop her! Avantika had advised against it. I should have listened to her.'

'She didn't want Palak to go with me? *Why?*'

'Avantika likes you. But Palak has a boyfriend, and we didn't want something to go wrong. Avantika thinks you sleep around!'

'Firstly, I don't sleep around and, secondly, I didn't know she had a guy,' I said in my defence.

Sleep around? I had not dated anyone in more than a year now. I was too involved with Mom, and the last girl I had dated was in school and we broke up when she shifted to Australia for her graduation. I had had *crushes* on girls, but things had not worked out. I had been too preoccupied.

I remembered, when I was fifteen, Deb used to tell me stories about all his flings and relationships. All this was before Avantika came around and straightened everything out. Avantika was an incredibly beautiful female. I still have the text Deb had first sent me when I asked him about Avantika after their first meeting.

She is so hard to describe, Benoy. Those limpid, wet, black eyes screamed for love. There is nothing better than a melancholic beautiful face. The moonlight that reflected off her perfectly sculpted face seemed the only light illuminating the place. Somebody was standing with a blower nearby to get her streaked hair to cover her face so that she could look sexier managing it. She had the big eyes of a month-old child, big and screaming for attention. A perfectly crafted nose, flawless bright-pink lips and a milky-white complexion that would put Photoshop to shame. Oh hell, she is way out of my league. She is a goddamn goddess. I just could not look beyond her face. I think I am in love.

He has been in love ever since. I envied him. Deep down, I wanted something like what he shared with Avantika.

Deb was the one who had exposed me to relationships, make-outs and flings, and he was often surprised at my *non-existent* love life. He often thought that I was lying. Since he had slept around back in his day, he thought I had done that, too. Deb often said that if he had my kind of money, cars and everything else, he would be dating Deepika Padukone. But then again, I was not that rich. I did not own an airline. Or have a British accent.

Chapter Four

'What happened?' I asked Eshaan. I had picked him up from his house that day. He had called me more than twelve times that morning so it had to be important. He was tense and his face was red.

'I am sorry,' he said. 'There is a problem.'

'Now what did *I* do?'

'Nothing, it is all my fault,' he said. 'Can you drive a little *faster*?'

'Fine, but at least tell me what did *you* do?'

'You know we have a subject—macroeconomics and foreign exchange?'

'Yes, yes, I do,' I said. 'The old, skinny professor . . . what about it?'

'That old, skinny professor left the college and a younger one replaced him. He was a director at some management college before this, so he is extraordinarily strict. He divided us into groups and assigned us project work.'

'So? I am in your group, right?' I said.

'Yes, you were, but not any more. Diya, the group leader, sent the list to sir without adding your name. We have the presentations today, and all the other groups are full.'

'I don't have a group?'

'Yes.'

'And how important is this presentation?' I asked him, still not taking interest.

'He said he would fail or pass students according to their performance in this presentation.'

'Can he do that?' I asked.

'Yes.'

'Fuck,' I said. 'So can't I just stand with your group and tell him there was a miscommunication. Anyway, one of the groups had to have one extra member, right?'

'I talked to Diya and she refused. You know how she is,' he said.

'No! I do not know *how* she is,' I said, frustrated. 'I don't even know *who* she is!'

'Don't worry, we will talk to her. If not, we will talk to sir.'

Eshaan was back in his element. It was my problem and he was still using the word '*we*' as if it was his problem as well. We reached college and headed directly for our class. It had been really long since I had last gone there.

'Who is Diya?' I asked Eshaan as I scanned all the faces.

'There,' he pointed to a girl who was excitedly explaining something to a group of students.

I walked up to her, with Eshaan right by my side, and said, 'Diya?'

'Yes?' she said. 'You are?'

Diya, as I later learned, had topped the class last year. However, she was not happy about it because she had not made it to the university toppers' list. She was sixth on it. It was a terrible *tragedy*. Ever since she had joined college, she had had a one-point agenda. She had to get into the London School of Economics (LSE) with a full scholarship. She was the *geek* queen and she looked like it—dull clothes, big spectacles and her curly hair all over the place, the perfect picture of a full-scholarship student.

'Hi! I am Benoy,' I said. 'I was supposed to be in your group.'

All the students around her looked at me strangely. *Man!* These guys did not even know I was a part of their class. I could have asked Dad to get me through this class as well, but I wanted to avoid calling him again at any darned cost.

'Your name was not on the list. *We* are already seven people,' she said. People in her group nodded obediently.

'But, Diya?' Eshaan said.

'Yes, Eshaan?' Diya countered sternly.

For the first time I saw Eshaan a little off his game. Usually, given Eshaan's fair, cute, kid-like face, no one really argued with him but Diya did. Diya's voice boomed at him and it was arrogant and confident, as if it came from amplifiers in her throat. She stared directly at the two of us, like a witch, and we were scared as shit. I have never felt at home with intelligent and confident women; they have never found me funny or smart. Why would *anyone* love them? They only make you feel stupid and inadequate all the time.

'I had mailed his name to you and you said you would put his name in,' he argued.

'And I replied that I would look into it. I checked and we were seven students in the group already. I mailed the work division to all the members. You should have checked that then,' she almost said it as if it was Eshaan's fault.

In the back of my mind, I was already feeling terrible because it seemed I would have to ask my dad to *buy* this professor too. I was proving to be a very expensive kid.

'Okay, there seems to be some misunderstanding,' I said. 'I will just stand with the group when you give your presentation. We will tell him that we forgot to put my name in. What about that?'

'What? Benoy, right?' she said, clearly not looking pleased at my idea. 'Look, I am the group leader and I was responsible for sending the names to sir,' she had now started tapping her finger vigorously on her laptop, 'and I will not accept that I did something wrong.'

Diya had really started to piss me off. Little Miss Perfect.

'Fine then. Let Eshaan be the leader then. He will accept the mistake,' I said.

'Yes, I will do it,' Eshaan said.

She looked angry now, her nostrils were flaring and her eyes were bloodshot. I guessed she had burst a nerve or two inside. I wanted to step back a little. Just in case.

'Why?' She said, '*I* did all the work and what if sir asks questions? I will not put the whole group at risk just for *you*.'

I was almost shocked at how nerdy and headstrong this girl was. I did not know what to say.

'C'mon, Diya,' Eshaan said.

'*What?* I just won't allow it. Now, if you are done, we have to revise,' she said and looked away from us.

'You know what?' I said and she looked at me. 'You can take the project and shove it up your tight ass for all I care.'

I cannot say I was not scared as I said that. It looked like she would throw her laptop at my face. Thankfully, she did not. I did not want my face to get any uglier. I walked away. As I strode outside the class, I could hear Diya shout at Eshaan and tell him what a horrible guy I was. I did not care. Well, the others in the group just asked, *'Who is he? Never seen him in class!'*

Chapter Five

A little later, we all sat in the class, and she was still right there. Her nostrils still looked like caves and the big eyes behind those spectacles looked at me as if they were trying to blow me up. She had a striking resemblance to the lizard on the ceiling that watched me just as she did.

'So, what do we have lined up for today?' the professor asked. He was younger and he definitely looked sharper than the other professors who taught us.

'Project presentations,' one of the students said. I have never understood *these* students. Why do they have to go ahead and remind teachers that they had to screw us?

'I am glad you remember them,' he said. 'I went through all of them. How do you guys think you did in your projects?' he asked very harmlessly.

The answers ranged from *okay* to *good* to *could-have-been-better*. I looked at Diya with a cold stare although her eyes were stuck on the professor. Freaking nerd girl.

'Good? Excellent?' he said, smiling. '*PATHETIC!* Just *pathetic!*' he shouted suddenly.

I had always considered that my ears were impervious to any nonsense from teachers and professors, but this professor was loud. Windows shattered, guys pissed in their pants and people broke out of their daydreams.

'Do you call *those* unformatted pieces of shit *presentations*? I cannot believe this is the state of affairs at one the most prestigious graduate colleges in India. No wonder you guys never make it to management colleges and those students from engineering colleges do. *DISGRACEFUL!*'

He started to hurt where it hurt the most. No commerce student wanted to be compared to an engineering student and be told that he or she was less intelligent or brainy.

'But, sir,' Diya interrupted, 'we—'

'Diya, right?' he said. 'You think *you* did any better? All you did was copy-paste from websites. Only numbers! Where was the analysis? I asked for a study. What did you think your numbers meant? *Who* all were in the group with you? Stand up,' he shouted.

Everyone in the group stood up, and I stood up too. I wanted to add salt to Diya's wounds. I wanted to make it worse for her. I wanted to stomp on her. Bloody *lizard*. The professor looked at all of us. He counted. The veins in his eyes had turned red and thick in anger.

'Eight of you?' he said. 'Wasn't I clear enough that one group wouldn't have more than seven people, Diya? You were the group leader, right? *Terrible.*'

'Sir,' her voice was now not even half as confident as it was before, 'he is not a part of our group.' She pointed towards me like a little school-going child.

'You are not?' He turned to me. 'I have never seen you in class before. Do *you* even come to college?'

'I had some problems at home,' I said.

'Anyway, what is *she* saying? Are you a part of this group or not?'

'Sir,' I explained, 'I was a part of their group but she kicked me out without informing me and I did not know when this presentation was. So, I didn't take part in the presentation too.'

'And you say it's *her* fault?'

'No, sir, it was mine, too. But I was meant to be a part of this group,' I said, as politely as I could.

'NO, he was NOT!' she shouted, and though the class was shocked at her loud outburst, it almost brought a smile to my face. I could almost see tears in her eyes. *Yes!* I pumped my fist. *Take that, bitch. Lizard. Bitchy Lizard.*

'Shut up, you two. Look at the two of you. What do you think this is? First grade? Everyone in the class will repeat their projects. You will choose new topics and I will send you the guidelines this time. And *you two*, yes, you will form a new group and only you two will work on the project.'

'But, sir? I cannot work with him,' she protested. 'He doesn't even come to college. He is irresponsible and brash.'

She stood there, helpless. Her desperation was extreme. *Life is so fair.* She was now stuck with a lazy, incompetent guy! *Oh, that's me. Shit.*

'That's not my problem,' he said. 'Although, Benoy, please don't think that your dad can make a call and you will pass this subject. That will *not* happen. Do you get it?'

Fuck him. Life is so unfair. Later, he added he could ask either of us to present and we would be marked as a group.

Therefore, if I were to screw up, Diya would get a zero, too. It was a foolproof plan to screw us up. He said he would ensure the external examiners did not score our final papers.

For the rest of the period, he kept harping on about how disciplined and intelligent students are in IIT Delhi, the college from where he graduated. He said he was appalled at the quality of students outside colleges like the IITs, DCEs and NITs. He was pissing off everybody in the class. *Up your ass*, I wanted to say.

I should have been worried but I was happy that the arrogant girl got screwed with me as well; her shoulders had drooped and her face had lost its colour. As soon as the class ended, Diya started to look for me. I hid behind a big group of students and left the class with them.

Fuck her, but yes, I was scared too.

Chapter Six

I would not say I hated him but I did not love him either.
I was just indifferent.

It was one of those unpleasant days. I strode inside
Dad's office. Every month, I had to sign a few papers, agree
to a few deals and some other nonsense. Since last year,
every business that was in Mom's name was transferred
to mine and my signatures were required for every major
decision in the company. I waited for fifteen minutes in
the conference room for him to turn up with three of his
lawyers like he always did. Finally, he came and, as usual,
he was sharply dressed in a grey suit that fit him snugly
and a thin, black tie that looked smart on him. There were
no signs of a middle-age paunch. He hardly looked like a
father of a twenty-year-old.

He was almost as tall as I was. Black hair peppered with
white, a hint of stubble, dark brown eyes and exactly my
complexion. I could bet my money he looked better than

I did. Secretly, I had always felt good when relatives said that I looked exactly like my dad.

Like every big business person in Delhi, he had never been to college. He took three attempts to clear school. He started as a minor steel trader in Sadar Bazaar, but slowly and steadily, he rose to become one of the biggest manufacturers of heavy machinery in India. He did it for the big industries, the government and the army—the people that mattered. My mom, a double doctorate in contemporary literature, told me that she was dejected because the man she was getting married to did not even understand the language she spent so many years studying.

Things had changed now, though. As his business grew, he had to deal with high-profile clients and so he had mastered the language. He had spent a major chunk of the last three years in his London office. He had come back with a hint of a British accent. He was now an older Indian version of Gerard Butler or George Clooney. Seeing him today, it is very hard to believe that he almost did not make it through school.

I always thought the real reason why these meetings were so painful was because I felt drawn to his charm. And whenever that happened I felt guilty about it since he had made my mom go through a lot. But when he stood in front of me, with an apologetic look on his face, and used compelling words, I had a tendency to forgive him from the inside. In those moments, I felt like I had *betrayed* Mom.

'Sign these.' One of the lawyers showed me where all to sign. I did not need to read those papers. He could not have possibly bought my forgiveness through them. I finished signing those papers, and the lawyers left.

'Benoy,' he said.

'Yes,' I tried to be unresponsive and cold. I tried not to look at him.

'How is college?' he asked. 'Have you started going?'

'Yes, as if you don't know,' I said sarcastically.

I knew he always kept tabs on me, tracked me wherever I went and knew whatever I did. I always thought he had someone following me at all times. Once, when my car broke down in the middle of nowhere, an employee of his was 'coincidentally' in the area to help me out.

'Are you interested? Do you like the subjects?' he asked and tried to be all fatherly. I wanted to tell him that it was too late to ask.

'I don't know. Some of them maybe,' I said, still trying to be at my rudest.

'If there is anything you need, you can always call me. And I was wondering if you would like to do your internship at my office in your summer vacations? You would get to learn a lot here,' he said.

'I don't want to,' I said.

Fuck! He even knew that I had been looking for an internship. It was something that we had to do after our first year. Usually, nobody took it seriously and everyone sourced fake certificates. But, I had spent months sitting at home or at hospitals and I thought the internship would be a welcome change. I had to be around people again! Life had sucked for quite some time. Things had changed a lot from my schooldays.

My school life was awesome! But now . . . every friend had got busy, moved out and settled in their college life. I was the one left out. It had been more than a year since I had any social life. Anyway, I had given a few interviews and had met with no success. At some levels, I always thought my dad was sabotaging my interviews with various companies.

'It's your choice at the end of the day,' he said, '. . . but you can think about it.'

'Fine,' I said and I got up.

His office was definitely much bigger than the offices where I had given my interviews. The only concern was whether I would be okay working with him. The more I thought about it, the more I was convinced that I *should* work with him. After all, he was my father.

Yet, my insides were tearing apart. On the one hand was my tendency to pick up the broken pieces of my life, have a sense of family, and on the other, it was hard for me to forget what my mom had gone through while bringing me up alone and my missing dad's part in all that.

I am too young to have to take these decisions, I thought.

Chapter Seven

*L*aw. Probably the most boring subject ever made. I have heard lawyers earn a lot. They deserve it, man! The torture they go through is unimaginable and no amount of money can justify it. Anyway, a really old professor was teaching us something and Eshaan probably regretted that he had called me to college that day. He called *ten* times that morning.

I was not letting him study. I did not understand why he was so diligently taking down notes. There were just lines after lines of text that one had to mug up and reproduce in the examination. As commerce students, we were *good* at that!

'How is Sonil?' I asked him, just to tease him.

'She is good. She really wanted to meet you that day,' he whispered, even though the professor had no real intention of stopping anyone from talking.

'Really? Why?' I asked him. 'I know she hates me.'

'She doesn't hate you,' he said, 'but she doesn't approve of what you *do*.'

Sonil, too, like everyone else thought I was a flirt and I put my hands (or something else!) on any girl that I could find. Initially, I used to get agitated but I had got used to it. Now I really did not care that much.

'Let's meet her today then?' I said.

'I have to go somewhere. A family friend's kid wants to know which stream he should pick. I got to go to their place ...'

'How come you *always* find things to do?' I said.

Like really. Eshaan always took special interest in other people's matters and all this kept him pretty busy throughout the day. When I first saw him in college, he was just another guy to me. Five feet eight, with a kid face, which instantaneously turned red in the sun. However, his energy and the forever-busy look on his face were some things you could not possibly miss. He kept hopping from one place to another.

I did not like him at first but he took a liking to me. I was like a charity project for him. A *misfit* in the college classroom. I could imagine what a kick he must have got out of helping me!

'Before the next class, just go and meet Diya once. She was looking for you,' he said.

'Me?' I asked. 'Why?'

'You haven't started the project, have you? You *ran* from the class that day, too! She was pretty pissed at you,' he said.

'Bitch.'

I looked at her and she was sitting where she always sat. The *first* seat. She furiously jotted down everything that the professor had to say. She looked at the professor with unwavering concentration. I admired her patience and dedication. The class ended and the old man crawled out of the class. He said something about an assignment but nobody gave a shit and everybody moved out. Diya still sat there and underlined her notes. *Nerd.* As Eshaan left, he asked me to go and talk to her. I did not want to. I was sure she would bombard me with questions, abuses and responsibilities. I wanted none of these!

I slowly trudged towards the first seat. I wished the ground beneath would open up and I could walk into hell rather than into a conversation with her. I went up to her desk, smiled at her and hoped she would not give me much work.

'Sit,' she said politely. Even then, I feared her reptile tongue might appear and suck me in.

'Is there any topic you want to work on? Or do you want to go ahead with the topic that sir gave us?'

Maybe, she was not a pain in the ass after all.

'No, let's do what he has asked us to do. We are anyway a little screwed,' I said.

'Good then,' she said and bent over on the other side. She was searching for something in her huge bag and finally took out a book. *Free Trade Agreements* by some goofy-named author. Though the name was not what I was concerned about. I was concerned about its thickness! It was almost as thick as my forearm. *No way!* I shat my pants.

'So . . . err . . . What do we do with *this*?'

'Umm . . . nothing much,' she said sarcastically. 'We just need to read this, then critically analyse this *book* and give our own suggestions. That's it.'

Now she did not sound as sweet. Arrogance and sarcasm came rushing back into her voice. I heard the sentence again in my head. *Read the book, analyse it and give suggestions.* The stupid, fucking professor wanted us to read the entire book. And trust me, it's not that I cannot read, but this was not a novel; it was a thousand-page book on economics and we had to go through the *entire* book.

'But this isn't even in the course?' I protested, as I flipped through the book.

1256 pages. Small font. I would rather be eaten up by Diya. Make her a reptile, please.

'Isn't it, Benoy? Then I will just go and tell sir that you think it is out of the syllabus and you don't want to do it,' she said coldly, adjusted her huge spectacles and looked away.

Every time she looked at me, her face distorted in hatred and repulsion. The feeling was mutual.

'I never said that,' I said.

'Then?' her voice was now meaner and colder, like a pissed off schoolteacher on a low salary.

'I will read it,' I said and tried to sound as harsh as possible.

'Fine, read the book by day after and then we can discuss it. Note down anything that you think is important. Okay?'

'*Okay?* What okay?' I said. 'Just two days? At least give me a week? Please?'

I panicked. Anyone would. *1256 pages? Two days!*

'We don't have a week, Benoy; he wants us to submit an initial framework in three days. And he might want to meet us tomorrow,' she said, collected her things and was about to leave.

'Is he crazy?'

'I don't know, but he certainly thinks we are *dumb* and if you mess this up, I am going to the principal,' she said and looked at me with those unrelenting eyes.

'Fine,' I retorted and looked her back in the eye. Well, I would be lying if I said I was not a little scared to look at her like that.

'I will see,' she said, 'you undeserving brat.'

I think she wanted to say that in her mind, but it came out. She left without saying another word, leaving behind an air of hatred and just plain disgust.

Undeserving brat.

I did not have a comeback for that. I was taken aback at the unnecessarily vicious comment. She was being a *bitch*! Now, I just *had* to finish the book and do it before her.

I called up Eshaan and he said he would have loved to help me out but he was caught up. He apologized more times than I could count. I disconnected the line, stared at the book that lay on my table and cursed the professor. *Argh*. My mind had started weighing options—call up Dad and ask him to write a big cheque? Or read the 1256-page book? The first option seemed more lucrative.

I was staring blankly at the book for what seemed like ten years when my phone rang. Strange. *Palak calling*.

'Hello?' I said, not sure what to expect.

'Benoy?' she said. 'What's up?'

'Umm . . . nothing much. How are you?'

'I am fine,' she said.

She did not sound half as cheerful as she was that day. I did not have a crush on this low-sounding girl on the other side of the phone. I had it on the girl who had been drunk and happy and danced as if she were nuts.

'Is there something wrong?' I asked.

'No,' she said. 'It's just that . . . my boyfriend . . . he told his mom about me.'

'Umm. Okay,' I wondered what that had to do with me.

'So, I was thinking if I should tell him about *us*.'

'About us?' I asked. 'What's there to tell him about us?'

'That we spent the night together, Benoy.'

As soon as she said that, I started wondering if we had actually made out. It seemed so now.

'But I passed out as soon as I reached home,' I said. 'Didn't I?'

'But what if you hadn't?'

'If I hadn't? Even then, how would things have changed?'

'Something might have happened,' she said. 'That's why you didn't drop me at my friend's place, right?'

'Umm . . .'

It was a hard question to answer; I had not dated or got anybody home in a long time. I could not predict whether I would have done or tried doing something with her. I mean, it was not that I had not fantasized about doing that, but ... well ...

'I don't know,' I said. 'I don't remember anything about us that night. What did I say? What did I do?'

'You remember nothing?'

'Nope.'

'Benoy, on our way back you were being very sweet to me. You held my hand and said you had had a great time and you didn't want to drop me at my friend's place. So, you asked me to come over. And stupid and drunk as I was, I did so! *Stupid me.*'

'Okay.'

'I came to your place!' Palak said, 'I have to tell him, right?'

'No, you don't. Look, Palak. Nothing happened. And that's what matters.'

'Umm ... Benoy?' she said. 'You sure?'

'Most certainly,' I said.

'You don't *like* me?' she said.

What!

'I do like you, but,' I said, 'we don't know each other.'

'You must think I am so stupid, right?'

'No, Palak, you are cute. And I had a huge crush on you!'

'*Had?*' she asked naughtily.

'Umm ... still do!'

'I like you, too,' she said. 'And who knows, if I didn't have a serious guy, I might just have done something that night. *Whatever.* But, thank you!'

I could see her smile from the other side. I am sure I *had* a crush. I liked her better when she was hard to get.

Random make-outs with committed girls only lead to troubled hearts and unwanted tears. It's what people always expect of me, making me even sure it's something from which I should stay away.

There's no glory in a fling.

Chapter Eight

I did not study the entire night.

My ex-girlfriend from school and I talked on Skype through the night. She told me about her new boyfriend, and I felt bad for myself. She had gone to Australia for her graduation. We had broken up a few weeks after she landed there. The initial days of separation were cool. For the first few weeks, we let our hormones decide what we did on the video chats. Skype was the best thing to happen to long-distance relationships.

However, slowly the lust, the stripteases, the role plays died down; things changed and we knew it would not work out.

I got up late the next day and opened my book. And Face*book*. Time flew by! Two hours and I had managed to go through just ten pages. I was not making any progress. Frustrated, I drove down to college to study there. I picked out a corner table in the library to hide from the embarrassment of being in the library.

I called Eshaan but he was busy helping that witch, his girlfriend, fill out examination forms. I put my head down and started to study and within moments, I was staring at the ceiling, looking at a lizard, which looked back at me with its gooey eyes, reminding me of *her*.

I attacked the book with newfound vigour. This time, an hour passed by and I covered a substantial portion. I only understood parts of it, but I kept going. Just then, someone tapped on my shoulder. For a second, I thought the lizard had fallen off the ceiling on to me. But it was *worse*.

'How far have you reached?' I knew that arrogant tone. It was Diya.

'Huh? Oh. Hundredth page.'

'How do you think you're going to complete the entire book? He might call us today! How can you be so careless, Benoy?'

'And will he ask us questions, too?' I asked nervously, the little nerd in me surfacing. In school, I used to beg and run after teachers for that extra half mark.

'*Yes*, Benoy, we have to go and meet him,' she said, as she put down her books on the adjacent chair.

As if on cue, the professor appeared out of nowhere and tapped on both our shoulders and asked us to follow him. We looked at each other and were somewhat scared. We followed him into his room.

'So,' he said and whirled around in his chair. We kept quiet. He was not a very pleasing man. He exuded hatred and always sounded angry.

'Have you read the chapter on US foreign policy yet?' he asked. It was the second chapter of the book. I had just finished reading it. However, the professor looked at Diya. He wanted her to answer it. *Darn!* He should have asked me.

'Umm . . . err . . . yes, sir,' she said.

'So tell me, what was different about NAFTA? Something that was not done by the US earlier?' he asked and leaned forward. I knew the answer. I looked at Diya and she was sweating like a pig. I wondered why because she had already read it. She was way past the second chapter.

'Umm . . . sir . . . it was the . . . first . . . time . . .' she mumbled something.

'*What?* I cannot hear you, Diya. Be a little loud. You were pretty loud when you shouted at him. NOW?'

She gave it another attempt, but she just kept stammering and mumbling nonsense.

'Don't waste my time,' he said.

'Sir—'

'Have you even *read* it, Diya?'

It looked like she would burst into tears. She kept quiet and stared at her feet. She had seemed pretty belligerent and confident that day, but in that room, she couldn't answer that simple question.

'Sir,' I said. She was close to tears. I was a little shocked. I started to feel sorry for her.

'Yes, Benoy.'

'Sir, we had divided the chapters. I was supposed to do it and explain it to her,' I said.

'Is it? Then you tell me the answer to the question.'

I launched into a monologue and answered it perfectly, much to the surprise of both Diya and the professor.

'Fine,' he said, 'but in the final presentation, I can ask both of you anything. Do I make myself clear, Diya?'

'Yes, sir,' she purred.

'You can go now,' he said and pointed towards the door. We left.

~

It had been two hours since we left the professor's room. Diya had been sitting just two seats away from me but we had not exchanged a single word. I was bored; Diya was still revising the second chapter, underlining with the ferocity of a rabid dog.

'Diya?'

'Yes?' she said.

'You forgot the answer?'

'I have been studying all night. I was exhausted. I don't know what happened inside. I just went blank. It was written right here! In my notes,' she said and held her head in her palms.

'Do you think I can share your notes?'

'I think so. That's why I made them,' she said.

'You made them for *me*?'

'I didn't want *you* to mess it up but *I* messed up.' She felt ashamed.

'The main presentation is what matters.'

She was a little less cold now. It did not look like she would make my brain explode and splatter on the back wall, with her stares. She handed over the notes and sat down next to me. Just as I was scanning through the notes, she said, 'And don't mix up the notes. I have marked the pages too, if you need to go back to the book.'

I nodded like an obedient child and started flipping through the notes. I have to admit, I was insanely impressed. Not only were the notes super precise, they were also comprehensive. *Incredible* handwriting. The indentations and the colouring and the diagrams, it was awesome. I closed the book and started reading through the notes.

I took breaks to see where I had reached in the book and the progress was phenomenal. I needed a break but Diya's concentration reminded me of ancient sadhus' and I didn't want to be the dancing apsara who usually jinxes it.

Tired, I finally asked her, 'Coffee?'

'Why? It's just been two hours?'

'Exactly. It's been *two* hours.'

'You go. I will finish up this chapter first.'

'I will wait then,' I said and sat down, thinking it would be rude to go.

'It will take an hour,' she said and looked at me. I am sure she saw my face droop because she added, 'Okay, let's go now.'

I hadn't noticed earlier, but now I couldn't miss her pyjamas and the faded, loose T-shirt. It was taking the I-come-to-college-to-study-and-not-to-walk-on-a-ramp attitude too far.

'Thank you,' she said, 'for helping me out.'

'Oh. It was nothing,' I said, 'and thank you for the notes.'

'I was helping *myself* out, not you. I didn't want you to put me in any further trouble,' she said. I thought we were past the being arrogant stage, but it seemed like we were not.

'Why are you being so rude?' I asked.

'Rude? Me? Look who's saying that! The spoilt brat with a silver spoon,' she exclaimed.

'Here I am trying to make things better and you are—'

'Make things better? I worked on that project for two weeks. And because of you, it all went waste! I don't want you to make things better. Thank you for helping me inside but that's it,' she said.

'Huh? But—'

'We don't have to be friends. We will never be. I do not like you as a person. In fact, I *hate* you.'

'What did I do?' I defended myself. The silence in the library was much better than this girl treating me like a doormat.

'Let's not have this conversation,' she said.

We made our way to the library and we were back to hating each other; she got back to her books and I got back to her notes. We did not talk to or look at each other. We were back to being sworn enemies. The clock struck five and I saw her pack her stuff inside her trademark big school bag.

'Umm. Can I take these?' I pointed to the notes.

'Sure. You can *shove* them up your tight ass for all I care,' she said and left the library, without looking back.

Crap. She remembered what I had said to her the first day that we had met.

You can shove the project up your ass for all I care.

I regretted my words.

Chapter Nine

The next day, I reached the library before time. I had thought about various ways in which I could apologize but I realized I was thinking too much. I picked the same seat that I had picked the day before. It was strange because I loathed her a day back and suddenly I was waiting for her in the library so that I could apologize and we could study together. *Diya. Library. Study. Sorry.* All these words were odd.

I was halfway through her notes when she came.

'Hey,' I said and smiled at her.

'Hey.'

She did not react. She unloaded her bag, took out about three books, a notebook, another set of notes and kept them on the table, two seats next to me.

'Umm, Diya. Listen, I am sorry about that comment. I really didn't mean it.'

'Okay,' she said and stared into her book.

'Like, I am *really* sorry.'

'Hmm.'

'So? I mean, do we still talk to each other like we want to kill each other?'

'We still don't have to be friends. Can we get back to the book? A lot is still left,' she said and buried herself in the book.

We got back to our books. I was not comfortable sitting with a person who was pissed off with me, but there was nothing that could be done. I was distracted thinking about it, so I logged into Facebook, searched, found her profile and added her.

A little later, I dropped in a message.

Nice profile picture.

Her phone beeped. *Oh shit.* She read it and kept the phone on the table. No reaction. I forced myself to concentrate on economic and fiscal policies, most of which made little sense. A little later, my phone beeped. It was a Facebook message.

Diya Gupta: Thank You. And I don't hate you.

I smiled, bent over and asked her, 'Coffee?'

'But I just got here. I think we need to study a little,' she answered, but I pleaded and she agreed.

We started talking again, and I kept my fingers crossed that I wouldn't wake up Cruella de Vil again. When she was not shouting or being arrogant, she really had a sweet voice.

'It was sweet of you,' she said.

'As in?'

'What you did for me yesterday. And the apology . . . It was sweet.'

'You didn't leave me a choice. I had nightmares of you stabbing me in my sleep.'

'I can't say I haven't thought about that,' she said. 'I am glad I didn't do it, though. But you always came across like an asshole. The big cars, that unabashed swagger, not a care in the world, sick attitude and that image of yours. You paid for admission and you buy out professors. It's not fair!'

'Hey,' I said, 'I paid for just two subjects in the first year. The rest of them were my honest attempts to learn on my own.'

'Really?'

'Yes, Eshaan taught me everything. What did you think? I paid for *everything*? Do I look that dumb?' I asked. We took our seats in the library.

'Well, I will not lie, but you kind of do look stupid in your stupid red shoes and your tight T-shirts.'

'Whatever!'

'But why didn't you just attend classes?' she asked.

'My mother was undergoing treatment for cancer last year so I had to miss a few,' I whispered, as the librarian motioned to us to stop talking.

'Oh, I am sorry. Is she better now?' she asked apologetically.

'She is dead,' I said flatly. I have never got used to saying that; it's still as painful.

'I had no idea,' she said suddenly, as she looked at me. I knew the look in her eyes. It said, *Oh, his mom died.*

'It's okay,' I smiled at her.

'I am sorry. I thought you lied when you said you had family problems.'

'C'mon, there was no way you could have known.'

I smiled and asked her to concentrate on the job at hand. I assured her that I was fine, and yet, she kept looking at me from time to time with pitying eyes. It was four in the afternoon when we took the second break. She was still on the thousandth page because much of her time went into helping me out rather than reading the book herself. I had slowed her down.

'I am sorry. You could have completed the book by now if I were not this dumb,' I said.

'C'mon. *We* are a team. And we are only as strong as our weakest link! And I didn't say you're stupid. I just said you look stupid,' she said.

'Whatever,' I said and sipped at my coffee.

We took frequent breaks and we gossiped about professors, our classmates, people we had crushes on (all her crushes were on senior toppers), and she was surprised to hear that I was single.

'Didn't you once date someone from the fashion parade team? During the very early days?' she asked.

'Naah, not really,' I said. 'Just rumours. I had just talked to her once. Did it become news?'

'Kind of.'

'You are kidding me! And then you say I look stupid. All evidence points to the contrary. I think I am gorgeous in my red shoes,' I said.

'You're so gay, Benoy.'

'You're just jealous,' I said.

'Yeah, right,' she said.

We went back to the drudgery of our books, and we laboured on till it was six and time for Diya to go back home.

'You can't go now! We have so much left to do,' I protested.

'Benoy, it will be seven thirty by the time I reach home. I am not allowed outside beyond that,' she said. 'You will be able to do the rest on your own, right?'

'On my own? There are two hundred more pages and you didn't even make notes for it!'

'Benoy, you can! Stop freaking out,' she said sweetly.

'Like I can climb Everest and design the next supercomputer.'

'Shut up,' she said.

'Please? You can come to my place and study!' I begged.

'Thank you for the invitation, but it's not possible. My parents will, like, literally kill me. Like they would actually chop me up and feed me to the dogs.'

'I wouldn't want that,' I said, and added, 'for the dogs' sake. I don't think you'll taste all that good.'

'Fine, then. I will just go and you can finish the rest WITHOUT MY HELP,' she said, faking anger.

'I was kidding, man. I'm sure anyone would love eating you. Okay, let's do one thing. Let me drop you home, and on the way, you can orally explain to me the chapters a little bit and then I will read it on my own.'

'But I am going home with my sister,' she said.

'So?'

'Okay, I will just call and tell her that she should leave on her own.'

We picked up our bags and headed towards my car, and she called me a lucky bastard after seeing the car I drove.

'You're so spoilt,' she said.

'I know,' I replied.

We hardly studied on the way back. She was too busy

poking fun at how rich and spoilt I was, and how poor she was, and kept saying that I should adopt her and the rest of the college.

'Here,' she said, as we stopped outside the decrepit government flats that seemed like they would fall apart any moment; the buildings were stained from the water that seeped through their walls, the paint was wearing off and the walls were scaly; they were a wreck.

'This is where you live?' I asked.

'Yes, right there,' she pointed to a balcony with clothes hanging on a clothesline, with a smile on her face.

As I saw her smile, I could not remember the last time I had smiled looking at my house after a long day. My house had a fully functional gym and central heating, while hers had leaking pipes and stained walls, and yet, she was smiling and I was alone.

'Thank you for everything today,' I said and got down from the car too after her. 'You are such an awesome teacher.'

'As if I had a choice. You're pretty clingy, Benoy,' she said.

'I have been told that. But hey, just one thing more, the bag you carry has to go! It's ridiculously big, Diya. It looks like you're carrying dead bodies inside.'

'If I had the kind of money you have, I would have slaves carry my bags, bags much bigger than this,' she mocked.

'Yeah, yeah.'

She left and I drove back home, smiling. Diya was not the kind of girl I was used to, but behind all the crappy clothes she wore, the hideous spectacles and the dead people's bag, she was pretty in her own special way.

I went back home and opened the book immediately

so that I could finish it up quickly before falling asleep. I revised what I had studied since morning. I was amazed at how much I could recall. I felt intelligent!

I called her. She was busy making the presentation. In the background, I could hear her entire family shouting and creating a ruckus.

So, that's how a family feels like, I thought.

I couldn't study for much longer, and I logged into my Facebook account.

Diya Gupta accepted your friend request.

She hadn't uploaded many pictures on to her profile, but she looked nice in the few she had. She would have looked much better if she got rid of her spectacles and brushed her hair once in her lifetime.

However, it was not her pictures that kept me occupied for the rest of the night. It was someone else's.

~

I woke up the next day, a little groggy from the previous night, tired, because I had just fallen in love. I was still hugging the laptop for dear life.

It wasn't her pictures that kept me up all night, but someone else's. Most of those were not tagged so initially I did not know who *she* was, but I felt compelled to find out. I started scanning through her friend list. *Once. Twice. Thrice.* None of the faces matched! Well, there were 687 friends and a lot of them had decided to hide their faces with flowerpots or replace their faces with Japanese schoolgirls with striped stockings. There was no way I could tell *who* that girl was.

Well, the girl in the pictures was *beautiful*. It seemed like that girl's eyes would pop out of the screen. She was fair and she had such extremely sharp features that could cut through steel, yet soft like a kitten's. Facebook pictures often lied, but it was such a beautiful lie.

I wanted to call Diya up and ask her about *the girl*, but it was not a wise idea! I didn't want her to think I was a creep who spends nights staring at pictures of random girls and tries to establish contact.

But, I mean, there has to be some law against looking so *perfect*.

It was only after I read a few comments on one of the pictures, in which the girl had a cute puppy pout, that it struck me who she was. I felt stupid for not having read the comments earlier.

Diya Gupta: Well, thank you. After all, she is my sister. <3

Almost immediately, I ran the search '*Gupta*' in her friend list.

Bingo!

Shaina Gupta. Studies BA (Hons) English at Miranda House, Delhi University. Lives in Delhi. Knows English and Hindi. Born on August 12.

Her picture was a sketch, but it was a *match*. It was *her*. Diya's sister. I had slept with Diya's sister. I had hugged the laptop to sleep!

Shaina Gupta. I already had a big Facebook crush on her.

Chapter Ten

Diya and I spent the next week studying and fine-tuning the presentation, ironing out the chinks and revising the course over and over again.

I had not stopped stalking Shaina's profile, her blogs and her sketches (there were many!); if there was any trace of her on the Internet, I got to it and devoured it. Her poems were mostly distressing, in a silver-lining sort of a way—a dying girl meeting God, a hurt puppy getting wings and other weird magical stuff—and her sketches were either of beautiful girls crying or sitting on the edges of cliffs or they were dressed up in finery, holding wine glasses in hand; it was confusing and intriguing, and I couldn't make out if she was a depressed alcoholic or a pretentious prick.

Diya and I gave the presentation, and it went beyond our expectations. Well, she was *horrible* when she started—she sweated, rubbed her palms together, faltered and forgot everything. Diya totally blanked out again and the professor just made it worse by raining down a flurry of questions on her.

'What was in that slide again?

'You have written this here, but earlier you said that . . . ?

'Can you explain this slide?'

She had looked at me when she was all lost. I looked at her and smiled. She smiled back at me. I think that gave her confidence because little by little, all her nervousness evaporated, and she kicked some serious ass out there. The professor, surprised and defeated, turned to me and started asking me questions.

'So, Benoy, now you tell me . . .'

Only God could have bettered my performance.

The professor accepted that when he announced the grades and said that we had far surpassed his expectations. *Fuck him.*

I was glad it was *over*.

'Happy?' I asked when I left the class. She had been freaking out all day, like only girls can, as if tension-inducing hormones are girl-specific.

'You have no idea how much, Benoy! I had been so tense. You did so good!' she said and hugged me again. She could not stop smiling.

'Yeah, I have to admit. I was kind of awesome.'

'You're so full of yourself!'

'But you kicked ass, too, Diya,' I said and smiled at her.

She was ecstatic. I was happy because she was so happy. It really meant a lot to her. I was glad I had been a part of it.

'We should go out and celebrate,' she said.

'Kamla Nagar?' I asked.

'Only if you're paying,' she said. 'I mean I shouldn't have to tell you this. It's been days since we had food on our table at home. I'm starving. I think I have goitre and beriberi. I am, like, the poster girl for malnutrition.'

'Shut up! You're not THAT poor,' I said.

'You never know,' she said and we laughed. She couldn't stop making fun of the economic chasm between her and me. We went to the closest coffee shop and I couldn't get her to stop talking. She didn't let me pay so we split the bill.

'So you're saying your parents will get you married as soon as you graduate?' I asked. 'But who's going to marry you? Won't people notice the bag you're carrying?'

'He he. Benoy, I know you think you're funny, but you're not,' she mocked. Then added, 'They will not get me married if I, like, get through to London School of Economics on a full scholarship for my master's.'

'LSE? You will go to London? I'm not sure if they would let those spectacles inside their country,' I responded.

'Fine. I just hope I get the scholarship. They just choose two out of thousands of applicants. I wish I could sell a kidney and scrounge up the money,' she said, despondent.

'But are you serious about the marriage thing?' I asked.

'Dead serious. You have no idea how conservative my dad is. He would get me off his back like this,' she answered and snapped her fingers. 'It's so unfair. Benoy, I have not dropped out of the top five in any grade. In ANY grade, and I didn't study hard all these years to be a housewife at twenty-one. It's just not fair.'

I nodded, not knowing what to say.

'Best of luck,' I said. A little later, we left the coffee shop and walked to my car.

'Diya,' I said, as we huddled inside the car. 'There is something I wanted to give you.'

'*Me?* What?' she asked.

'Aw! Benoy, you didn't have to do this,' she said, as I gave her the bag I had bought for her. 'This is too small for carrying the heads of the little children I kill every day!'

'Can you stop being disgusting for a minute?' I grumbled.

'But I do not need this. You need this. You don't have a bag.'

'I don't have a bag because I don't need one! I don't want my best friend to look like the Hunchback of Notredame with that bag,' I said.

'Don't push it. I am NOT your best friend,' she retorted. Seeing me make a puppy face, she cupped it in her hands and said, 'You're, like, my only friend!'

'That's better!'

'You are sweet, Benoy.'

'Thank you. You aren't bad either,' I said.

We smiled and though she was happy, I could not ask about Shaina, something I thought I would. I thought she would pick up the conversation because I had liked *every* picture in which she was with her sister, but she did not mention anything.

Chapter Eleven

'Where the hell are you?' Deb asked.

'I was in college. Why?' I said.

'College? Just when I need you, you are in college? Come home, I am outside. And why college, man? Is everything all right?'

I wanted to tell him that I enjoyed attending classes with Diya, but I couldn't mouth the words; I couldn't even believe the words.

'Why? What's the problem?' I asked because I had never seen Deb so flustered.

'I need to do something special for Avantika and I thought I would decorate your house and get her here. What say?'

'Deb? Haven't you already done that before, like, a million times?'

'But that's all I can think of. I have done almost everything else. I don't know what else to do, Benoy.'

'But it's not her birthday, right?'

'Will you just stop attending your stupid classes and come home?' he asked.

I excused myself and hurried back home; Diya told me she would photocopy the notes for me.

'What's the matter? Why the big surprise?' I asked as I let him in and he sat on the couch, his head in his palms.

'I am tired of the cat-and-mouse game, Benoy. The pursuit and everything have lost their charm and I want to get it over with.'

'Get it over with?'

'Yes, Benoy, get *engaged*!' he said. 'Do you even have any idea when was the last time I made out?'

'Umm . . . a year ago? Is that why you want to get married? That's the stupidest reason ever!'

'Well, not really, but that could have been playing in my subconscious, now that I think. Anyway, I really need her, man. The break-up is killing me now. She used to be everything to me. She was the person whom I could fall back on. Now it just sucks. Don't you wish for someone like that in your life?'

'I already have that someone in my life. *More* than one.'

'Benoy, I am really not interested in listening about your flings right now,' he said. I was talking about Diya and Eshaan, and I would never make out with either of the two!

'Whatever,' I said.

'Anyway, I will do it with a big diamond ring, and I will get it soon,' he said.

'Umm, okay. I am not sure if it's a good idea,' I murmured.

'What? You think I shouldn't do it?'

'No,' I said. He looked at me and wanted me to explain my apprehension. 'Look, Deb, you have cheated on her. *Twice*. That's not by accident. You're an asshole.'

'So? I won't do it ever again, Benoy. I love her,' he protested. 'And there is no one else I could ever get married to. You know that! I love her too much.'

'It hasn't even been a year since you two have been apart. Give it time, maybe you will get over her. It's not the first time you're breaking up with someone!'

'I don't want to get over her,' he complained.

'I know, Dada, and, well, I like Avantika, but you know you shouldn't get into something like marriage without being sure,' I argued.

I was never against relationships, but I had seen Mom in a loveless marriage.

'Benoy, I know why you're saying this, but not every marriage breaks down,' he continued.

'I read somewhere, *All weddings end in either divorce or death. Nothing good can come out of it*, Deb!' I coaxed. 'Plus, if you get married, I will lose a brother. I can't have that! You're the only family I have, man.'

'C'mon, Benoy. I will always have time for you. You just have to call and I will be here.'

'Oh, fuck off. Either you're busy in your business or busy wagging your tail around Avantika. I'm not even sure she likes you any more,' I ranted.

'Of course she likes me!' he scoffed.

'Do whatever you want to do! Why did you even ask me?' I barked.

'Because you're the only one who understands. Dad

can't care less, and Mom wants me to marry a Bengali girl,' he reasoned.

'I am on your mom's side,' I said. 'And you're so young, Deb. Like, you're twenty-one!'

'I'm twenty-five,' he countered.

'You look twenty-one!' I exclaimed.

'I just want to know you're with me on this one,' he said.

'Fine, whatever. Don't run after me when she refuses and tells you that she has a boyfriend far better looking than you.'

He laughed.

With Deb engaged, I would need a girlfriend at least. He left my place after an hour. Nothing I said could change his decision. He was going to do it, much to my disappointment.

Once he left, I switched on the laptop. Shaina had posted three new poems on her blog. I couldn't understand one of them. I suspected the leaking boat in the poem was a metaphor for life, but I wasn't sure. The other two poems were just twenty lines long, and I cursed when I finished reading them in a few short minutes; her sentences always had a tinge of tragedy sprinkled in them—honest and beautiful. Like her.

And I had not even met her.

Chapter Twelve

Over the last few weeks, there had been two people who had been extremely happy. One was Eshaan. The other one was, well, me! Eshaan saw me in college every day and now he could go a little easy on project '*Help Benoy*'.

Diya and I were growing close. Diya was fun and bitchy and really mean when she wanted to. The *look-at-her-boyfriend* type. I had slowly dragged Diya from her traditional sit-on-the-first-bench-and-write-everything approach to listen-to-only-those-professors-who-matter approach.

The best part about her was that she smiled and laughed at whatever I used to say. She made me feel that I was the funniest guy in the whole world. It was a great ego boost. I liked spending time with her; she was insanely funny, and she laughed at all my jokes (that was new!). After a long time, I had found someone like that, like a breath of fresh air.

'This is so boring,' I whispered in her ear.

'Shut up,' she said, as she jotted down something that the professor said.

'HEY!' the old professor shouted and looked at us. He warned us to stop talking or he would throw us out of the class. I wished that he would, and the next time he caught us, he did.

'I told you to SHUT UP!' she said angrily.

'I did! It was you who was talking. You asked me to shut up and that's when he caught us.'

'But I had to ask you to! You just keep on talking like you have something important to say but all you say is bullshit,' she said, as she angrily walked towards the parking lot. I was laughing and that was pissing her off.

We instinctively went to the coffee shop we used to go to. Her anger fizzled out in a while. We figured we could not remain angry at each other for long. We were back to our usual conversations, and she began to analyse me like a certified psychiatry practitioner, something she loved to do.

'But how can you make out with someone you barely know, Benoy? That's disgusting,' she snapped.

I had told her about my friends, all of whom were rich and slept around. My school life was pretty happening. I had a serious girlfriend, but all my other guy friends were good-looking and popular, and they led scandalous and colourful sex lives. In fact, the school basement was out of bounds during our last year in school because our headmistress had caught two of my friends having sex with their girlfriends in the music room in the basement, together. It was a huge scandal!

Diya refused to believe I wasn't one of them.

They did this to ensure privacy!

'It's their personal choice,' I said. 'It's their lives. Let them do what they want to. It's not as if they are doing it in your bedroom.'

'Don't lie! I am sure you did it too. Serious relationship, my foot! You seem just the kind of guy who would do such a thing,' she accused.

'Why don't you believe me!' I said and refreshed the browser on my phone. Shaina hadn't uploaded anything new.

It was very important for me to drive it into Diya's head that I was not as bad as she thought I was, that I was not a flirt, and that I didn't sleep around. It was bad enough that I was stalking her sister on Facebook. Tired of trying to convince her that I was the good guy, I steered the conversation away from me.

'Why do we always talk about my relationships? Why not yours?'

'Mine? Be serious, Benoy. Who would date me? I am every guy's worst nightmare. And plus, my parents would have killed me had they known.'

'Oh c'mon. You haven't dated anybody?' I asked.

'Umm . . . I have . . . one. Two, really. It's pretty daring of me to do so. I felt like Lady James Bond, and I had to be all sneaky when I used to meet them. I don't date now. I don't want to break their trust in me. I was young and foolish.'

'Aha! This is interesting,' I said. 'So tell me *everything* about the guys!'

Her first relationship was in school when she was in tenth standard and they were together for two years. After school, he went off to do his engineering from somewhere outside Delhi. And as it happens, differences crept it. Different schedules, different timetables, new friends and new insecurities. Not to forget, expensive STD calling too!

'Long-distance relationships don't work,' she sighed.

'I know. My ex-girlfriend went to Australia after school,' I said. 'We used to Skype or use video chat on Yahoo! for a few days. But, it didn't work out!'

'We used to Skype, too!' she exclaimed.

'Aha! And do *what* on Skype?'

'Shut up!' she said and looked away, smiling. It was hard for me to imagine Diya acting naughty on the webcam. It's like imagining kittens having sex. There's nothing sexy about it, and it's totally wrong. The only things I thought she would sleep with would be books, notes and exam answer sheets. If anything, maybe a picture of a professor.

Her second relationship was more of a fling, even though she never admitted it. It lasted just a month. The guy was in Hans Raj and thought Diya would be an easy lay. *But Diya? An easy lay?* Well, whatever.

'So, it was really a fling!' I said. 'I can't believe you fell for the guy. You are too intelligent for that shit.'

'I'm a girl too. And the smartest of girls get their hearts broken by the dumbest of guys,' she snapped.

'Yeah, behind those spectacles, I really can't see anything.'

'Whatever you might say, it wasn't a fling. Now, shut up,' she said.

'So? Who was better in bed?' I asked.

'You cannot ask me that. And I asked you to shut up!' she said.

'I can,' I said. 'You said that day I can talk to you about anything.'

'I meant about *you*, not about *me*. And this conversation is over. You can't ask girls that question. This is the reason why you're single, Benoy.'

'I'm single because I choose to be single. You know I won't let this go. You got to tell me.'

'Okay, fine, it was the second one,' she said.

'The one you had a fling with? You dirty girl! Did you get in a leather dress and whip him too?'

'It was not a fling, Benoy! And leather is too expensive. I'm the rich dad's son after all,' she snapped.

'Okay, whatever. So you had a better time making out with the one you were in love with just for a month,' I said, just to drive it home.

I pressured her to tell me more, but I got the feeling she might kill me and stuff my head in that old bag of hers, so I backed off.

But? Still? Diya? In bed?

'You look positively shocked, Benoy. You thought there wouldn't be a guy who would want to make out with me?'

'Are you crazy?' I said. 'No! You are very pretty. Any guy would like to make out with you. I don't know *how* that's a soothing thing to say, but no, you are nice.'

'You don't have to lie now. You think I'm odd, don't you?'

'I like odd,' I corrected.

She was not bad looking. Diya was even cute, but I was never attracted to her like that. And when I told her she was cute, she blushed like a schoolgirl.

'But, Benoy, you must have had flings, right? You don't have to lie to me. I will not judge you.'

'I am not like that. Why do you keep saying so?' I asked.

'Benoy, you are okay looking in spite of your stupid shoes and the big cars. You look like you must be dating many girls at one time. Girls like Palak—they must be falling all over you.'

'Hmm,' I said, not wanting to clarify. I was pissed off even though this was not the first time. Deb, Avantika and now even Diya made me feel that the only reason a girl would ever date me was that I was rich and connected.

Diya was the last person whom I wanted to think that. I had been obsessing about her sister. Her poems were becoming darker, and there were more sketches of women and girls crying and staring at the setting sun, which I now knew from her poems was a metaphor for oblivion. The silver linings were getting thinner; I was concerned.

So finally, I decided to pick up the conversation. Diya had uploaded a few pictures of herself with Shaina and I had liked them.

'By the way, the new pictures, I like them,' I said.

'Hmm. I saw you liked them. Thank you! You should spend less time on Facebook.'

She had missed the point *again*! How could she miss it again? In all other matters, she was all brainy, but why miss this! It was frustrating.

Anyway, we were drinking our coffee, when I was patted on my back. It was Eshaan and his scrawny thin *girlfriend*, Sonil. I wanted to throw up on her.

'Not in class?' Eshaan said.

'Obviously not,' I said.

'Hi, Diya,' Eshaan said and looked at Diya.

And I looked at Sonil and smiled. She was unmoved. *Bitch*.

'Why don't you join us?' I asked, even though I did not want that scrawny, painfully thin, tall bitch anywhere near me. She was taller than Eshaan and not cute at all. Eshaan deserved someone cuter, someone more like him. Someone like Diya! They were perfect!

Eshaan and Sonil sat down and they ordered for themselves. Sonil and I repelled each other like similar poles of a magnet.

'So, why here?' Eshaan asked.

'He got us kicked out,' Diya said.

'Ohh. Eshaan has got kicked out because of him a lot of times too, though it gives us a lot of time to date,' Sonil said. I am sure she meant it as a joke. Ha ha. *Nobody found it funny, bitch. Moral victory, yeah!*

'So, Sonil, what do you do?' Diya asked her.

'Maths Honours. I plan to take the IAS exam after this.'

'That's great. Lots of money, I have heard,' I said.

'It's not the money. It's the respect that matters,' she said and looked at me as if she had been starving for months and I was a juicy burger.

'Yeah, but there is a lot of money too.'

'For your information, it's a government job and no government job pays well.'

'But there are other sources of income!' I said, purely meant to poke fun and nothing else.

'You think every administration person is corrupt? No. It's because of you businessmen who try to buy our honesty, dangling your stolen income in front of us, that we stray,' she grumbled.

'Firstly, I am not a businessman! And everyone knows why people become IAS officers. No one respects IAS officers. They respect the money they have,' I said, and now I wanted to scratch her face open.

'It's narrow-minded people like you who bring the country down. Buying professors, buying government servants.'

'So then ask them not to get sold! If I can buy it, I will. It is up to *you* whether you get sold or not,' I said and she frowned.

'Whatever,' she responded. 'You're from the filthy breed of rich people who think they can buy anything and anyone.'

'Okay, fine, I am like that. Let's not get into this any further,' I said.

'Yes, let's not,' Eshaan said. All this while, Eshaan and Diya were just watching us bash each other.

'Why not, Eshaan? I do not know *how* you are friends

with someone like *him*! He only uses you. Attendance, talking to professors, assignments . . . that's all he needs you for. Can't you see that? Why would he ever be friends with *you*? Has he ever done anything for you?'

'Umm. He drops me home sometimes,' he stuttered.

'At least I don't try and control him,' I said.

'I do it because it's for his own good. So that he doesn't waste his life on friends who don't give a shit about him. To keep him away from suckers like you,' she bawled.

'I think you should go,' Diya interrupted and looked at Sonil and handed over her bag.

'And you, Diya—'

'You should go,' Diya said, '*or it will not be pretty.*'

'Fine,' she said, grabbed her bag and Eshaan, and got up. 'But listen, guys like him are parasites and you will know that soon. *Humphhf.*'

She walked off, leaving us in an awkward silence.

'Such a bitch!' Diya said after a while.

'I know,' I said. 'But you were good! Especially with that dialogue—*or it will not be pretty*! It was awesome. But just curious, what would you have done? Catfight? Eh? Tear each other's clothes off?' I joked.

'I don't know. I just get a little possessive about people close to me,' she said and smiled at me.

A little possessive? Little? In those moments of *it-will-not-be-pretty*, it seemed like she would drive a fork through Sonil's eyes. I thought it would be best to delay the question, '*Hey, is that your sister in your pictures?*'

'Anyway, you didn't tell me, did you give that second guy

a blow job? Tell me now or I will tell your parents that their daughter goes about giving blow jobs to men!'

'Fuck off.'

~

Eshaan called me later that day to apologize.

'I am very sorry about Sonil today,' he said.

'It's okay, Eshaan. I know she doesn't like me, no big deal. But why don't you dump her! She is such a bitch. Why can't you see that? She treats you like her puppy, man.'

'C'mon, I am lucky that she is dating me,' he said and he was adorable when he did that. 'I am not *you*, Benoy.'

Argh! Not again.

'Any girl would love to have you. You are cute!'

'You think so?' he asked innocently.

Eshaan was the perfect guy to date. He looked cute, was sincere, considerate and caring. Just the guy a girl would like to tell her friends about. Or even her mom, for that matter.

'Yes, I think so. Why don't you dump her and date someone who really deserves you. Like . . . umm . . . say *Diya*?' I said.

'Diya? I thought you were kind of—'

'NO! We are just friends. C'mon! You know me better than that,' I clarified. He fell silent. Eshaan was like an open book. It was child's play to guess what he was thinking.

'Do you like her?' I asked.

'Not really,' he said. 'She is nice . . . but no. Maybe. She *is* cute.'

'Fine, fine,' I said. 'You can figure that out later, but please break up with that girl. And for heavens' sake, do it soon!'

He laughed about it, and bitched about Sonil; I hoped Eshaan would realize how wrong Sonil was for him.

Chapter Thirteen

Deb had not yet found the perfect ring, and he had been everywhere in Delhi to look for it. He had even called his ex-girlfriends and Avantika's friends to help him out with the selection of the ring, but he just could not choose one. That day when my phone rang and I saw Avantika's name flashing, I wondered if Deb had found the ring and proposed.

'Hey,' she said.

'Hi, Avantika! Long time.'

'Yes, how are you? Are you and Palak still . . . you know?' she asked.

'No! Not at all. Never met her after that day.'

'Aw. Sad for you. Anyway, I wanted to ask you something about Deb. He is behaving a little strangely.'

'As in?' I asked and put the phone on loudspeaker.

'He is a little too *happy*, Benoy. He doesn't call as often and is always busy. It's been quite a while since he asked me to patch up with him. It's so unlike him.'

'So why are you so worried?'

'I am not worried. I am happy for him. But then . . . Okay, Benoy, I will ask you something. Please don't lie to me.'

'I won't!' I said.

'Has he found *someone*?' she asked in all seriousness.

Only God knows how hard I tried not to laugh when she said that.

'I don't know and I am not lying.'

'I am so sorry, Benoy, to drag you into this. I am just scared that I might have pushed him away. I should not have made him *wait* this long. I should have patched up.'

'Chill, Avantika.'

'But what if he is *with* someone else? I even saw his messages on a friend's phone. I could not read them but he *never* texts my friends. Why did he text *her*?'

'Why are you getting so scared? This is what you wanted, right? You always asked him to look for someone else since you could never see him as your guy again,' I argued.

'I never thought he would go away. I just wanted him to run after me a little more! It's not that he has not tried to make me jealous before, but this time, I feel something is up.'

'You are thinking too much, Avantika.'

'I don't know. Did he tell you something? *Anything?* He must have talked to you?'

Deb, who was sitting with me, had listened to the entire thing on loudspeaker, smiling stupidly like an orang-utan. I felt happy for him.

I assured Avantika that she had nothing to worry about and she disconnected the call.

'Benoy, don't you think marrying her right now would be a little too drastic? We can *wait*, right? As you said, I'm still young!' Deb said and smiled.

'You're such an asshole, Deb,' I barked.

'Chill, I'm not going to stop looking for a ring. But it's good to know that she won't reject me when I go down on one knee,' he responded.

'So happy for you, man,' I said and hugged him, and felt sorry for myself. He was convinced about the big steps he wanted to take in his life, and I couldn't even ask Diya about her sister.

Chapter Fourteen

I was at Dad's office signing papers that day.
Luckily he was busy in a meeting so he could not come out to see me. I signed the papers quickly and left the office. I smiled at the few girls that worked there. It was not that bad a place. I could have worked there for my internship. Anyway, I walked to the underground parking space and towards my car, my eyes darting to spot the car Dad used to drive.

The beautiful silver-grey Bentley.

I looked at it and wondered if there was anything that a man could want more. I walked past it, trying not to drool, headed to where my car was parked and beeped it open. I put the key into ignition and reversed the car out of its parking space, but the car stuttered, jerked a little and came to a rude stop. I shut the engine down and tried again.

Kharrr . . . Khaarhh . . . Khaarhhh.

The car stuttered for a while and came to a stop. I gave it a few more tries, pushing the pedal all the way down, but the car died on me again.

And then, there was smoke rising from inside the hood of the car. *Darn*. Frantically, I stepped out from the car and stood at a distance, just in case it decided to blow up; it happens all the time in the movies. I waited for the smoke to settle down. I stood there watching the smoke settle, and then tried to call a cab, but the network was terrible.

'Is there a problem, Benoy?' a voice called out. I wondered if it was Jack the Ripper, but it was my father.

'It died,' I said and pointed to the car.

It was still spewing out fumes. Diya would jump and dance and laugh if she were to see the car bathed in white smoke; she had been trying to make me use public transport instead. She was appalled to see how much I spent on fuel alone.

'The network doesn't work here in the basement,' he said. 'You want me to drop you somewhere?'

I considered it for a few brief seconds, and then thought, *What the heck*; at least I would get to sit inside the shiny Bentley. I felt like a cheap pervert as I looked at the car, wanting to take it out, get it drunk on diesel, drive her around town, to take its top off and stare at the bare V8 engine. I *lusted* after it.

I nodded my head and he tossed the keys towards me and said, 'You can drive.'

My hands trembled, my lips quivered, I sweated and blood rushed to every part of my body; it was an orgasm.

'Great car,' I said even though describing it as just '*great*' was an insult. It's like calling Lana Del Rey just another girl; it's like calling the Beatles a boy band.

'Your mother used to love this car a lot, too,' he said, almost mumbled. 'I used to be scared when she used to drive this.'

'*What?* Drive?'

'Yes. She never told you that she drove this car?'

'No, she didn't. All I knew was she didn't want me to have this car.'

I knew they met now and then, but I did not know that Mom drove his car. All I knew was that she hated him!

'She loved this car. I actually bought one for you but she didn't let me give it to you,' he explained.

'I know about that. I don't know why she would keep me away from something this awesome?' I said as I pushed on the gas, making the beast roar.

'She didn't want you to be anything like me. Or do anything the way I do it.'

'How does owning the same car make me like you?'

'That's exactly what I told her. But she just didn't listen,' he said.

I found it hard to put all this together. Like him and my mother talking about the kind of car I should get. I always thought that my hatred for him was a continuation of my mom's hatred for him.

'This is so much better than the Audi,' I said.

'You can keep it.'

'It's hard to say no to such a car,' I said. I felt like such a sell-out, a disgrace. It felt like betraying Mom, but it was she who was talking to him, not me.

'Then don't. Just keep it. Anyway, it takes up way too much space in my garage,' he said, like a salesperson, only that he was buying me; I felt worse.

'Thank you.' I sold. I could almost see Mom shaking her head, pointing a finger at me and saying, 'You're greedy.'

We reached Barakhamba Road where he said he would get down.

'Thank you for the lift,' I said.

'Thank you for the lift, Benoy. It's your car now,' he said and smiled.

'Thank you for the car.'

This was the longest conversation I had ever had with my dad.

Until I was seventeen, I had barely heard him talk, and I assumed, like all steel traders, he would sound like a rustic, uneducated businessperson. I had no idea that over the years he had made up for his lack of education and how! What I really hated about him was his British accent! I mean, how could he be *cooler* than me? That is never how a father–son equation works!

It was hard growing up without a father. But it was even harder to stay angry when you miss having a family, a family that could possibly have a *cool dad*.

I drove around in the new car for about an hour, testing its limits in the open wide roads, and then came back home. I parked the car outside my house and, out of habit, I pulled open the glove compartment for the house keys.

A *package* fell out. I emptied the glove compartment, collected the spare keys from the neighbours and headed home. I checked the boot space for stuff that my father may have forgotten there, but there was nothing. I dumped everything on the living room table and flopped on the couch, still fantasizing about the car. I called up my father's personal assistant to come and collect the stuff but no one picked up the phone. I dropped in a message.

I called up Diya to tell her about the new car.

'Hey!'

'You sound happy?' she said. 'What happened? Did your father buy you Russia or something?'

'You should meet me! Like right now? Can you do that?'

'I don't know. I will have to ask Mom. I will call you back if she decides to let me live.'

'Fine, do that and call me. ASAP.'

Diya had always had trouble getting permission to go out of the house. Her parents were a nightmare. No guys. No late evenings. No night-outs.

I waited for her call; intermittently I would look out of the window and admire the car in the parking space. I could not wait to show it to Diya, Deb or whomever I could have got hold of.

I called her again, but she cut my calls. Then, just out of boredom, I started sifting through the stuff I had got out from the car's glove compartment. I picked up the package, which was deliciously sealed, pasted and taped.

And until this day, I wonder how my life would have been had I not *opened* that envelope.

Chapter Fifteen

There are times in life when a few seconds change everything. Either you are irreversibly fucked, or you hit a jackpot, but regardless, nothing remains the same.

I had that moment then when I opened that envelope; everything changed. It was indescribable what I felt because I felt happy and sad and beautiful and cheated; I felt like crying, but I also felt like laughing.

I held the envelope and tried not to cry, a million questions in my head. I did not know what to feel. I felt lied to. Cheated on.

But I felt happy. I lay there speechless, on the couch, with the phone in my hand, and there was just one question I wanted to ask!

Why?

I called Diya again and explained to her what I had found.

'So what exactly are you saying?' Diya said, as I told her what I had seen.

'Hmm. You didn't get it? These are letters. Pictures. Even tickets to Sikkim. There was a micro SD card with pictures of them. *Together*. They looked happy. And this was not when I was eight or something. This was when I was fourteen, fifteen, and even sixteen. Even a year before Mom died. Together, the two of them . . . *they even went on a trip together*.'

'So?'

'What? So? It means she was still meeting him while I thought she was angry with him! What does all this even freaking mean? My mom kept talking about how bad a father he was, that he cheated on her, and these pictures?' I said.

Silence.

'The only reason why I was angry with my dad was because my mom was angry with him! But this . . .'

It felt like someone had pulled a nasty joke on me. I did not know what to make of all that. Wasn't I supposed to be angry and pissed off at him? I was supposed to stay away from him.

I was furious because I had missed out on having a family, a proper functioning family with both my parents together. This was just unfair. The picture of them by the river, in an upscale restaurant holding hands, the picture of them in a cable car. It really did not look like she was mad at him. They seemed happy! Mom looked happy in those pictures.

'Why don't you talk to your aunt?' Diya suggested.

'You think she would know anything about this?' I asked her.

'If anyone would—'

'I should leave then,' I said and picked up the car keys. I gathered all the pictures and other stuff and put them back in the envelope. 'Come with me, Diya. I can even show you then what I wanted to.'

'*What?* Wasn't this what you wanted to show me?'

'No! I will be outside your place in ten minutes,' I said and disconnected the call. She was waiting when I got there.

'What?' she said. 'You got to be kidding me!' she shrieked in pure excitement. 'I am sure your dad can buy Russia too!'

'Why the fixation with Russia?' I asked and she just laughed.

We sat in the car and left for Deb's mom's place. Diya *loved* the car.

'Benoy, are you sure I should come? It's your family matter,' she said.

'I want you around,' I said.

As I drove, my questions, my anxiety and my anger tapered down. I thought if Mom could forgive him, so could I. After all, I was not half as nice a person as Mom was. By the time I reached my aunt's place, I was sure that no matter what explanation I would get, I would forgive my father.

It was time.

~

'Beta?' she said, as she opened the door and I handed over the envelope. I touched her feet.

'Go through it,' I said and introduced Diya.

They both smiled at each other and she asked us to sit. She slowly went through all of it, alternating between looking at me and what was in her hands. She didn't look shocked. She just looked sorry that I had got to know.

'Who gave you this?' she asked, her hand on mine.

'That doesn't matter. What's all this?' I said. 'And I know you know.'

'I don't know what to say, Benoy.'

'You don't know what to say? I grew up without him being around because my *mom* asked me to stay away from *him*. Then what was all this? Trips? Dinners? Just tell me anything. Anything would do! Seriously. Tell me anything and I would believe you,' I said desperately, angry that I was the last to know.

'See, Benoy. I wouldn't lie to you.'

'Then tell me.'

'See, beta. It is not how you think it was. Your mother had a tough time dealing with your dad. He was nice when they got married, but then he got involved with his work, his business, and he just forgot he had a wife and kid at home. It was really hard for your mother. She used to cry for days on end. I saw her go through that. And with you, he just became *worse*. He wanted to turn you into him. He was strict and would even go about beating you, even when you were just a little kid. And that's why she left him. Not because he cheated, not because he didn't give her time, but because he was a very bad father to you and she couldn't take it.'

'I don't remember any of it.'

'You don't remember because your mother brought you up like that,' she said.

'But why this?'

'You know your father always kept tabs on you and

your mother. He still does. After your mother discovered that she had cancer, she didn't tell anybody, not even *you*. But your father, he knew. And he begged, he almost literally signed off all of his businesses to his partners just to be with your mother. Eventually, she forgave him, but she still wanted to punish him for being a bad father. What you have in your hands is their last times together. As husband and wife.'

'Okay.'

'It's not like how you think, Benoy. She always thought about you first. She just didn't want you to turn out like him, that's why she kept you away,' she said.

She clutched my hands, expecting me to break down into tears, and hugged me. I ruffled that package in my hands. I was not crying. I was smiling. I was glad that Mom had Dad around during her last days; she looked *happy* in those pictures, content. I had more to remember her by, and I was glad that she had a nicer time during her fading days. I knew she would not want anything bad for me.

I left her place in another twenty minutes, with the envelope in my hand and a strange sense of happiness even though I had just found out that my mother had lied to me about her relationship with my dad and kept me away from it, and I just got assured that I had a terrible childhood.

'That was sweet,' Diya said.

'What was sweet?'

'You cried.'

'*Me?* No! I didn't. I'm like Schwarzenegger in my head, buff and strong. I never cry—crying is for girls.'

'You had tears in your eyes.'

'Well, that and crying are two very different things. And the tears part won't ever be mentioned. It never happened,' I said, not looking at Diya.

'I thought it was very sweet to see you cry! At least it showed you have a heart,' she said.

'Emotional crap. I'm Schwarzenegger and the Hulk. I only get angry, not sad and weepy.'

'Whatever. I am glad you brought me along. I would have missed out on that. And your aunt is so sweet. Despite you being sad, she just couldn't stop offering me something to eat!'

I wasn't sad and weepy; I was just glad and amused. I mean there must have been times that Mom would have lied to me and secretly gone out on a date with her ex-husband, my father! *That is cute, isn't it?*

'Though, Benoy, I really don't get something,' Diya said. 'How can you be this *stupid*?'

'What stupid?'

'Do you really think that your car breaking down, your father offering you the car you have always liked in his parking lot and the envelope in the glove compartment of the car . . . do you really think all this is a *coincidence*? I do not think your dad is that stupid, Benoy! He *planned* it.'

Fuck. He planned it. Obviously.

Chapter Sixteen

It had been more than a week since I had found the envelope and the *secret* romance of my mom and dad during the fading years of her life. I had called my father's assistant and got everything delivered back to his office, after I made copies of everything.

'Did you call your dad?' Diya asked.

'No, I didn't. I just don't know what to say to him.'

'But you said you would?'

'I couldn't make up my mind.'

'Well, if it's too much of a bother, do it after the exams get over. Have you finished that chapter you had started with?' she asked.

'Umm ... err ... almost,' I said.

'Really?' she asked.

'Nope. It's so hard to concentrate!'

'Whatever. You don't need to study. This time, you can

just buy *every* professor. And prove Sonil true, you *good-for-nothing* brat!'

It was just a trick to get me to study and it worked every time. There was the *other* reason why I wanted to score well—the more pertinent one. I wanted to impress Diya and eventually ask her about her sister.

Shaina had stopped sketching, but her poems were getting longer, some even longer than a few hundred lines. Her words were as beautiful as she was, only more tragic.

Her last poem was about a little girl found in the rubble of a war zone, who walks about the city's ruins, looking for her parents and finding nothing but platitudes. I have never been big on emotions, since, as established, I was a curious mix of Schwarzenegger and the Hulk, but the poem had me bawling and crying like a little kid.

I was the little girl.

~

It was our last exam that day. The exams went well. Like incredibly well. There was an outside chance that I might even score higher than her. But then, even if I did, the entire credit would go to Diya for she made me work as hard as I had. Diya desperately wanted a university rank that year as otherwise her LSE dream would end then and there.

The best part about Diya was that she was like a girlfriend, but a non-fussy and a non-sexual one, which meant no possessiveness, no jealousy and no obligations. But she was always there when I needed her. These exam preparations just made me love her even more. She was so cute and caring, almost like a mini-*mom*, and that's why I always thought that Diya and Eshaan were perfect. They anyway treated me like their lost *kid*, so they should have started dating too!

'Hey, how did it go?' I asked Eshaan.

'Not so good,' he said.

His relationship troubles were haunting him. I partly blamed myself for it because I had put the first seed of doubt in his head about Sonil. But I never felt guilty about it. He had to get rid of that bitch. *Like. Really.*

'Any plans today?' I asked him.

'I got to meet her,' he said.

'Again? Didn't you just break up yesterday?'

'I did, but she just says something and we get back. She just doesn't let me break up. You were right, she is *very* dominating,' he said and I really felt sorry for him.

'Why don't you just stop taking her calls?'

'She calls on the landline, talks to my mom; things are not going well, Benoy.'

'Then tell her that you have started dating someone else? I am sure she will dump you then,' I suggested.

'She will ask for her number. What will I do then?' he asked.

'You are really scared of her, aren't you?' I asked. 'Tell her that you have started dating Diya! And I will ask Diya to say the same, what say?'

'Do you think Diya will do it?' he asked as his phone started ringing.

I told him that I would handle it and then bid him best of luck. I waited for Diya to finish her exam. She *never* left the exam hall until the last minute.

She left the examination hall smiling. Though her smile vanished in a matter of seconds when I told her that she might have to talk to Sonil and pose as Eshaan's girlfriend.

'It's just one call!' I said.

'You are so irritating!' she said. 'I don't want to talk to her. She's probably the last person I would ever talk to.'

We were still arguing about whether I should have done that, and how big a pain in the ass I was, when her phone rang and we knew it was Sonil. I snatched the phone, picked it up and handed it over to her as she kept trying to give it back to me.

Sonil came out all guns blazing, calling Diya a whore and home breaker and what not; Diya gave it back in equal measure, pulling out the choicest of Hindi expletives, insults that even I would think twice about. A girl swearing in Hindi is a dream; it's like a perfect picture of Women's Liberation.

'Not a word about this. *Ever*,' she said as she disconnected the call.

'You were good,' I whispered in her ear. I could see her smile, even though she tried hard to hide it. 'I have to say you were dirtier than the kids in the slums near my house. I need to treat you for this.'

'Benoy, I really have to go out with my sister today. I had promised her that I would. Tomorrow, maybe?'

'So what? Or do you have a problem if I come along? Anyway, I haven't met your sister. Oh, let me treat you guys.'

'My sister is sort of boring. I love her and all, but she's into sketching and writing really boring stuff. And moreover, I don't want guys like you hovering near her.'

'I am sure she's not boring,' I countered. I wanted to prove it by narrating the best parts of a few of her poems I had memorized.

'Fine,' she conceded. 'And don't blame me if she starts to talk about Byron and Keats.'

'I won't. And I love poetry!' I said. I only love *her* poetry; the only other poet I truly appreciate is Jane Taylor, the woman who wrote the twenty-line poem, but we know only four of the lines: 'Twinkle, Twinkle Little Star'.

We drove to her sister's college. Miranda House. Shaina was in her first year there. Diya and I did not exchange a single word. I was busy constructing sentences that I would say. Obviously, I could *not* have said, *I have been stalking your profile and your blogs obsessively, and I think you are like a beautiful flower, like a heartbeat—sensitive and beautiful.* I was nervous.

Will her eyes be as big as they were? Will her words rhyme? Will her hair be as perfect as it looked in the pictures? We reached her college and Diya got down from the car.

'I will just go pick her up,' Diya said and left.

I nodded and waited. As I sat in the car, I doused myself with perfume and checked my hair, and then I saw her, walking like she didn't know how unarguably pretty she was.

Crap.

This isn't the movies, I remember telling myself, but why had the people walking next to the car frozen in place and why did time slow down. I could only see her walking towards me as if I had blinders on. She was in a bright yellow T-shirt with a SpongeBob graphic on it, and bright green skirt-pants below, looking brighter than the sun.

I could see her smile from far. It was shy yet pretty, confident yet tragic. She resembled the girls in her sketches, beautiful and complex; the world seemed like it would end every time she blinked, hiding her big, brown eyes.

She reminded me of her poems, magical and complex, each feature of hers hiding a different story; her prettiness was epic and rich, just like the words she wrote and the sketches she drew.

She was not that tall, maybe five feet four, but those eyes, man, those eyes.

My heart thumped as she got inside the car, my breaths were heavy and deliberate, and I trembled. There was certain happiness in her prettiness, like she would smile and everything in the world would be okay.

'Hi,' she said. 'Shaina.' And she held out her hand for me to shake. I shook it.

'Benoy.'

'I know who you are,' she said and smiled wider. 'Nice car, by the way.'

'Thank you.' I blushed.

'He's just a spoilt brat,' Diya interrupted and punched me in the arm. 'Let's go?'

'Sure. Where are we going?' I asked.

'I don't know. I am okay with anything! Where do you want to go, Shaina?' Diya asked.

'Umm . . . I know you will kill me for this, but can we go to Pragati Maidan? The French film festival just started and they are playing *Queen Margot* today. I really want to see the movie!' she said, jumping in the backseat.

'French movie?' Diya said, disgusted. 'We won't even get a word of it! And your movies are so boring, Shaina. Can't we do something interesting for a change? Say like watching a Hindi movie that I would understand?'

'I am okay with it,' I said. 'I have never seen a French movie. I have heard they have, like, naked scenes and stuff?'

'Oh! Lots of them. Let's please go,' Shaina pleaded. 'I will translate whatever you don't get.'

'Whatever,' Diya said.

'You can understand French?' I asked, shocked and impressed.

'And Spanish,' Diya added. 'She is such a pretentious show off.'

'I don't say that when you talk about fiscal policies, do I?' Shaina quipped.

Shaina pushed me to drive faster because she did not want to miss the first scene of the movie, while Diya sulked, hoping we would.

They bought the tickets and I parked the car. Diya made sure she sat between the two of us during the movie. The movie was about a woman stuck in an arranged marriage during a period of religious war, and she hoped to flee with a new lover. Periodically, Shaina would make us understand the nuances of the story, and while Diya would shrug, I found myself staring at her, listening to her as she described in great detail the anguish and the pain of the woman in the movie.

I felt inadequate.

Finally, during the interval, while Shaina and I waited in line to buy popcorn because Diya said she would rather eat than watch the movie, Diya visited the washroom.

'So? Miranda House?'

'Benoy, that's a bad conversation starter,' she said.

'Let's see if you do better,' I said.

'I am equally bad at first sentences. But I really thought you would be arrogant and haughty. And yes, a lot uglier.'

'Uglier? Which means right now I am just ugly, not UGLIER?'

'No, no! I mean, you are cute. I thought you would be ugly,' she corrected.

'That's just damage control. But why did you think I would be even uglier?'

'Diya always said so! Don't tell her I told you this. She's a little possessive about me, so for her every guy is ugly and irresponsible. She's very protective.'

'I can see that,' I said and wondered what proportion of her face were just her immense, beautiful eyes.

Diya came back and asked us why we were smiling. We said nothing.

That little stolen moment between Shaina and me made my day. The movie ends with the beheading of the lover, and the woman, Queen Margot, lived on, carrying with her the embalmed head of her lover wherever she went.

We did not get to talk any more that day because they had to rush home as soon as the movie was over, but there were times that Shaina and I had longer-than-usual eye contact and we smiled at each other.

Chapter Seventeen

It had been exactly three days and I had not been able to push the thought of her out of my mind. I kept daydreaming about her, constructed fake dates with her, where I would just sit there and she would recite her poems, and tell me about her favourite movies.

My calls to Diya had tripled over the last three days because I wanted to hear Shaina's voice in the background somewhere. It just kept ringing in my head since that day and no matter what I did, it stayed there. It didn't take long for Diya to put two and two together.

'Benoy, one word about her and we will never talk again,' she said.

It was the millionth time that day that I had picked her name up in a conversation.

'I don't want you near her again. Do you get me, Benoy?' she said.

'But why? It's not as if I am hitting on her.'

'No, but you were staring at her! I don't want a guy like you hovering near her,' she said.

'Did she notice? That I was staring?'

'I didn't ask her,' she said.

'Did she say anything about me?'

'I didn't ask her that either,' she said. 'She is too simple for all your games, Benoy. And you know my parents. Please stay away from her.'

'Okay, fine. We will not talk about her.'

'Better,' she said.

No matter how hard I tried, I could not change Diya's perception.

'And you are not adding her on Facebook!'

'What's wrong with that?'

'Just like that. I don't want you to go about liking every picture of hers, like you have done in mine.'

'You noticed?' I asked.

'Obviously, Benoy. I am not blind.'

'Oh, okay. But—'

'Nothing doing. No adding her on Facebook,' she said this sternly, and we did not discuss it further.

Like a petulant child who does exactly what he's asked not to, *I sent Shaina a friend request.* The more Shaina was treated like a guarded princess, the more I was drawn to her.

My eyes grew weary and tired waiting for the friend request to get accepted, but I couldn't make myself give up on the hope.

And then, a message came.

Shaina Gupta: Are you sure? ☺ *Didn't Diya ask you not to add me?*

Chapter Eighteen

That day, Deb came over, and as if I was not already having a bad day, he had decided that he would add to my list of worries. I had spent an hour, and I had not yet drafted a reply. *Why the fuck can't she just accept the friend request?*

'Hey,' Deb said. 'Guess what?'

'That you're not getting engaged?'

'No, asshole. I got the *ring*!'

'This is the worst day of my entire life. The only brother I had is now someone else's. I don't have any reason to live.'

'Oh, cut it out and be happy for me, man.'

'Okay, fine. But have you thought this through, Deb? Being engaged? It is a big decision. No more sleeping around? No more night-outs or dates with other girls.'

'It's *the* easiest decision I have ever made. The only girl I want to be around is her,' he explained.

'That's sweet.'

'Yeah, anyway, you should be doing all that. Not me. *It's your time now!* I will just be the boring elder brother!' He smiled.

'I don't do that either.'

'Oh, c'mon. Don't be that boring, Benoy. I am getting engaged, and you seem depressed!'

'Okay, whatever,' I said.

We talked for a little while, and it didn't take long for him to notice that I was distracted. I kept checking the phone for a notification that would say that she had accepted the friend request. Maybe, she was waiting for me to reply to her message.

'I think I *like* someone,' I finally told Deb.

'Ohh, sure you do! Diya, isn't it? I always felt that. Even my mom told me that the way she looked at you at our place, she just knew something is going on. So?' Deb said excitedly.

'Diya? No. Are you out of your mind? I was talking about Shaina.'

'Shaina?'

'Diya's sister.'

'Diya's sister? As in, real sister?'

'Yes, real sister. What else?'

'Oh, that's just fucked up. Does Diya know?' he asked.

'I mean, she has an idea. And she doesn't like it.'

'Just tread carefully, Benoy. For now, can we stop talking about your girl? Okay, I will show you the ring, and even if you hate it, you have to lie. Get it?'

'Yes, sir. Deb sir.'

He showed me the ring. There was no way any girl would say no to a ring like that.

'It's brilliant,' I said and congratulated him again. I wished him luck and he left me to my misery. After he left, I went back to my message screen.

Benoy Roy: We don't have to tell her! ☺

It wasn't witty, it wasn't smart, but I had to reply.

Shaina Gupta: You don't but I have to. She is my sister! And she doesn't have nice things to say about you. ☺ *I don't trust men with big cars.*

Benoy Roy: She is just possessive! Will you add me already! ☺

*Shaina Gupta: *Runs to ask Diya if she should**

*Benoy Roy: Nooo! *Dies**

*Shaina Gupta: *Jerk**

A little later, I got the notification that I had been waiting for.

Shaina Gupta accepted your friend request.

Within seconds, Diya called. *Crap*.

'Benoy!' she almost screamed on the phone.

'You wouldn't believe what just happened,' I said.

'What!' she still screamed.

'Deb is getting engaged! He had this huge ring and he is proposing to Avantika . . . *right NOW*. Can you believe that? It's CRAZY!'

'What? *Really?*'

'Yes, he showed me the ring. It's *huge*.'

'You seem so excited,' she said. 'I'm so happy for him!'

'So am I!'

She was sufficiently distracted. We talked about Deb and

his engagement and what it would mean to me; she forgot she had to blast me for adding Shaina.

'But I had asked you not to send her a request,' she said, not as angry any more.

'When have I ever done what you have asked me to, Diya?'

We both laughed at it, and I mailed her the picture of the ring that I had clicked. She got busy with that. As soon as we disconnected the call, Shaina messaged me again.

Shaina Gupta: That was well handled! ☺

Benoy Roy: Anything to be in your friend list.

Shaina Gupta: That was creepy!!

Benoy Roy: The pressure to be smart and funny is getting too much to handle for me. What do you call creepy in French?

Shaina Gupta: Now that was sweet! ☺ *Creepy in French is 'rampé'.*

Benoy Roy: But you know what would be really sweet?

Shaina Gupta: I am thinking chocolate cake? What's on your mind?

Benoy Roy: Yeah. Chocolate cake. But yes, exchanging numbers!

Shaina Gupta: Why don't you call my sister and ask for it?

Benoy Roy: I think we should stick to chocolate then! ☺

Shaina Gupta: Aw! 9999993489!

Benoy Roy: So much better. ☺ *Vous êtes un grand!*

Shaina Gupta: Your Google Translate skills don't impress me.

And our conversation shifted from Facebook messages to text messages and when she had exhausted her free messages, I called her. She asked me to wait until her sister had drifted off to sleep.

'Hey,' I said.

'Hey, do you want to talk to Diya? She is right here,' she said.

'Very funny.'

'Why not! You're best friends after all,' she joked.

'Shaina, you are the girl here. I am the guy. I am supposed to be *funny*! And you are supposed to laugh at my jokes. Not the other way around.'

She faked a giggle and said, 'Does that work fine with you?'

'You need to work on making that giggle a little more realistic!'

We both giggled at this. This time, her giggle was more realistic. We didn't talk for long since she had an assignment to complete. Just before sleeping, I visited her profile and saw all the pictures again. I resisted the temptation to like all her pictures. I did not want Diya to notice that. And secondly, Manoj Nagpal, a guy from her list, had already done that. He had liked every picture of hers!

Manoj Nagpal likes this.

I checked him out, and he was a 'rampé'-looking guy.

Manoj Nagpal. Studied at Delhi University. Lives in Delhi. Knows English, Hindi and Punjabi. Born on September 12, 1986.

1986? Creepy *OLD* bastard!

Chapter Nineteen

'Has anybody replied yet?'
It had been quite some time since Diya had applied to a few places for a summer internship but she was getting nowhere with it. Unlike me, she was only sending applications to the top-notch organizations.

I had already given up and decided that I would work at my father's company. Despite fervent requests, she had refused help of any kind whatsoever.

'Nothing as of now,' she said.

'Do you want me to talk to my dad?'

'No!' she said.

'What if—'

'Eshaan called yesterday,' she interrupted.

'Aha! Eshaan? I didn't know you guys were calling each other and stuff.' I nudged her.

'He had called once to thank me for that day. I told you

about that! He said he was contacting a few companies and asked me if I wanted to apply.'

'I think he *likes* you.'

'No, he *doesn't*. He's just sweet and you know that.'

'I know he does. The question is whether you like him or not?'

'Like him? I hardly know that guy! And please, I cannot get into relationships like you do.'

'Why do you always say that? Have you in the last few months ever seen me talk about anyone? Or being with someone? This is unfair.'

'Fine. Fine!' she said.

'Seems like there are still a few things you have to know about me,' I grumbled. First thing amongst them was that I was in love with her sister.

'Oh. I totally forgot. I saw your dad's video on YouTube. He was invited to a conclave organized by the Chambers of Commerce,' she told me.

'What about it?'

'He sounds good! He has an accent and you don't. I am afraid but he's cooler than you are, Benoy. You're a step down in evolution. He's good-looking too. What happened with you? Are you adopted, Benoy?' she asked, smirking.

'Whatever.'

'I think you can learn a thing or two from him. He's quite the rock star,' she said. 'He's like the good parts of Richard Branson and Gerard Butler, and you're like the bad parts of Johnny Lever and the guy from *Frankenstein*.'

I stayed quiet; it was because I was happy and confused.

Chapter Twenty

The only time I didn't miss Shaina was when I was reading her blog and staring endlessly at her sketches. Calling her always daunted me because I felt like an illiterate homeless guy while talking to her. She was educated in French and Spanish, wrote poems and drew like a dream, and sometimes she would talk about poets and their lives and their best works, their techniques of writing and what not; I just drove around in my dad's stupid big car like it was mine.

'Weren't you with my sister all morning?' Shaina asked the first thing after answering my call.

'Yes, why?'

'That's creepy, Benoy. You spend all your day with my sister and then you hit on me. That's not done.' She chuckled.

'If I were hitting on you, I would have liked all your pictures . . . like someone has.'

'Someone?'

'Some guy. Manoj somebody in your list. He has liked all your pictures. Who does that?' I said irritably.

'Oh, c'mon. He's a nice guy.'

'And he is as old as your dad,' I snapped. 'He's twenty-six, Shaina. You are young enough to be his daughter.'

'Love knows no age!' she countered.

'You can like him as much as you can right now, but let me tell you, he's not going to last. A natural-cause death is fast approaching.'

'That's just mean. He isn't *that* old!' she countered.

'He is twenty-six! Imagine. When he was in first year, you were in the seventh standard. That's like paedophilia, Shaina.'

'Now you're just making it sound worse! George Chapman, a poet, said, "*Young men think old men are fools; but old men know young men are fools.*"'

'At least you agree that he's old. Are you dating him or something?'

'*Could* be! Could be not. Whatever be the case, I'm not looking to date you. You're not my type,' she professed.

'What's your type? I have already started watching all the top French movies in the IMDB list, and I am thinking of reading through all of Byron and Keats and Neruda and Frost, if that's what your type is,' I said.

'I think I should just go and tell Diya that you have been troubling me,' she jested.

'Err . . .'

'*Aw!* Look at you. You're cute, Benoy. I'm sure you will find yourself a nice girl. I am kind of surprised you aren't seeing anyone,' she said.

'I'm not!'

'I just thought girls would be clamouring to get to you. Except your shoes, I think you're everything a girl can ask for,' she commented.

'Is someone paying you to be sweet to me? I am really not used to it, Shaina.'

'Modesty! Thy name is certainly Benoy Roy. You know what, the first time didi talked about you, I thought she would explode! She was so angry, like really pissed off. What did you do? She told me that you were an inconsiderate, rich brat.'

'I am not a brat!' I protested. 'Oh, by the way, I loved the new poem. I don't know how much I got, but it's brilliant.'

'Oh, please don't read my poems, Benoy,' she said. 'They are horrible!'

'Are you kidding me? I have cried, like, so much reading them, and I don't even know if I understand them completely,' I said.

'You're just being sweet. No one really likes them. Everyone dies in my poems. How can you even like them? I don't even know why I write them in the first place. I end up depressing myself,' she explained. 'I want to stop writing them.'

'No! Don't stop. I love them,' I protested.

'Thank you,' she said. 'I think I should keep down the phone. Diya would want to know who I was talking to and I really don't like lying to my sister.'

We disconnected the call. It was a little uncomfortable hiding it from Diya. I slept peacefully that night, imagining Shaina in a quaint old town cottage, working on a poem in her study, while I looked on, thanking my stars for having met her.

Chapter Twenty-one

I sat there in my car and waited for her outside her college; I didn't think she would agree to see me without her sister but she did. I was ecstatic and nervous. The wait was long, painful and nerve-racking. She exited her college campus and our eyes locked. As she walked and smiled shyly, as she looked at me, I had to remind myself to keep breathing. I wish I had learned a few lines written by any French poet to describe to her how pretty she was, and probably impress her, but she knew I was an illiterate buffoon.

'Hi,' she said as I opened the door for her.

'Hi,' I repeated, voice barely escaping my throat.

'Don't you have a smaller car? This attracts way too much attention,' she complained.

'Umm, I think you attract more attention than the car,' I said.

'You never stop flirting, do you?'

I shook my head. I noticed that every time I complimented her she would curl up into a ball and be embarrassed about it, and then she would smile.

She did not have much time on her hands, and we were together just for the time it took for me to drive her home.

'I'm so embarrassed that you read my poems, Benoy. You must think I am some depressed widow or something,' she said.

'Not at all. I told you I really like them,' I said. 'I think you're just fishing for compliments.'

'No, I am not,' she said. 'Are you this sweet to everybody?'

'Not really, I just prepare my speeches for you.'

'Stop being so sweet to me, Benoy. You should try your speeches on someone else. I am really not looking to date anyone right now,' she conceded, and looked out of the car window, sad, like the protagonists of her tragic poems.

'Why is that? Am I that undateable?'

'No, with this big car and stuff, you are way too dateable. I am sure you're a heartbreaker,' she said.

'I will never do that,' I said, 'to you.'

'You never give up, do you?'

I shook my head.

'It was nice meeting you today, Benoy,' she said as we reached close to her apartment.

'The pleasure was all mine.'

We shook hands and got off the car. She walked away from me, and it seemed like the world came to an abrupt end.

~

I called her as soon as I got home; it was desperate but I couldn't help calling her.

'You need to stop calling me, Benoy.'

'Hello, nice to talk to you too,' I said.

'If Diya finds out about this, she will kill you.' She chuckled.

'Let's kill her first then?' I suggested.

'Wait. Let me just do that,' she said and added after a pause, 'okay, done.'

'So did you kill her?' I asked her.

'Yes,' she whispered. 'She did struggle a little, but I was stronger than her. I made it look like an accident. She slipped on the bar of soap and landed head first on the butcher's knife. I am sure no one will suspect foul play. It's the perfect murder.'

'You're deliciously entertaining, Shaina,' I said.

'Um, Benoy. I had wanted this for long. So I was already slowly poisoning her. But, today I couldn't take it any more. So, I just used the kitchen knife.'

'You know that you're totally random, Shaina? Right?'

'I know,' she said and laughed.

'I just called to tell you that I really liked seeing you today,' I confessed.

'I liked seeing you today too. The best part was when I got out of the car and I turned around a blind corner and I could see you, but you couldn't see me. I really liked that,' she conceded. 'Hey? Can you hold on for a bit? I need to get inside my blanket . . .

'Okay, I am back,' she whispered. 'I hope you can hear me.'

'It works for me,' I said and found myself whispering too.

'You can speak normally, Benoy, unless of course, you have someone sleeping beside you too.'

'Not really, but if I whisper like this, it will make me feel that I am there with you,' I said.

'I don't know what to say to that. You have all the arsenal to have girls running after you,' she responded.

'They don't work on you,' I said, despondent. 'What will work on you?'

'Stop trying on me. Don't you think I deserve better?' She chuckled. 'Ohh, call waiting,' she said and switched to the other call before I could say anything. I waited for fifteen minutes and then cut the call. It took Shaina about half an hour to call me back.

'Are you sleeping?' she asked. 'I'm sorry. It was an important call. Did I take too much time?'

'Thirty-four minutes.'

'You were counting?'

'Every second,' I said, trying hard not to sound pissed off.

'I'm really sorry. You shouldn't have waited,' she murmured.

'I can't help but wait.'

'Please don't be sweet to me, Benoy. You scare me.'

'Scare you?'

'You know you're charming and cute, but we need to maintain our distance,' she explained.

'Who was it?' I asked on an impulse, wondering why she always pushed me away saying things like that.

'Manoj.'

'Ohh, he is not dead *yet*? Last heard, they were looking for coffins his size.'

'Stop being so mean to him. He isn't that old.'

'Okay, but you have booked a seat in the old-age home, right?'

'Shut up!'

'But what is he doing hitting on someone half his age? Well, I forgive him! Anyone would hit on you!'

'See, there you go again.'

'With what?' I asked.

'Stop flirting with me! I have a hard time explaining to Mom why I smile so much these days.'

'That sounds good.' I beamed.

'I don't like you making me smile!' she said.

'You do the same to me!'

We talked for an hour, tucked inside our blankets, whispering into our phones, as if we were together, she and I, hiding from the world.

Chapter Twenty-two

The late-night talks with Shaina became a daily routine. But sometimes it was distressing because I had to fight for her time with Manoj Nagpal, the old creep in her friend list. And I was not winning the fight. Anyway, that day I was supposed to meet Diya. It had been a few days and we had not talked or met.

I missed her, but I missed her sister more. Yeah, yeah, I am an asshole. So what! Everybody loves their crushes/girlfriends more than their friends. I was no different!

'Someone's got too busy!' Diya said as I walked up to her.

'Me? No? You are the one who's busy giving interviews.'

'I don't have a wealthy father, Benoy. What was the last thing he bought you? A helicopter?' she teased me.

'Haw! That's just unfair.'

'I wasn't serious. But I have to give these interviews. Otherwise, my profile would look so empty,' she said.

'Anyway, where is Eshaan? Didn't he have his interview, too?'

'Yes, he did. But he had to rush home. He is always so busy,' she said, irritably.

'You seem upset that he's busy! What's up between you two? Something that I should know?' I said, grinning stupidly.

'Benoy, I really don't think of Eshaan like that.'

'But he does. He really likes you.'

'I can't worry about relationships right now. My father is a feudal lord,' she said.

'That's like the worst joke ever. And who said relationships and careers don't go hand in hand? Both of you love your books! Economics! And God knows what all! This is so meant to be.'

'If you like him so much, Benoy, why don't you date him? Stop pestering me about him.'

'Fine, I won't,' I said. 'Anyway, how's Shaina?'

'She is good, why?'

'Just like that. She ever mentions me?'

'You? Why would she mention you? I have said this before, I am saying this now, and I will keep saying this . . . you don't have to think about her. She is my sister. There are millions out there. Go after them!'

'But, I—'

'No buts. I said it. And that's final.'

I wished there was some way I could tell Diya that my feelings for her sister were genuine. Shaina and I had now gone on three dates. And I had to lie to Diya every time we had gone out. It wasn't the best feeling in the world.

Chapter Twenty-three

I had been counting hours. It happened every time Shaina and I had to meet. The nervousness, the confusion about what I should wear, the insecurity about my hair, new pimples . . . it made me feel like a little girl.

'Hey!' I said as I spotted her. She wore a bright red kurta, with jeans that hugged her shapely legs. She wore flip-flops; she looked just the kind who would go watch Spanish art movies alone and write depressing poems that people would discuss years after she's gone.

'You look awesome,' I said.

'Thank you. You look great too,' she said.

'Where do you want to go?' I asked, half expecting her to drag me to a library or a museum.

'We need to talk,' she said.

She sounded serious and we picked a place that was quiet and serious. It was very unlike Shaina, but I was positive. Maybe I would get to tell her today how much

I loved her; I had practised the speech a million times in my head.

'I talked to your sister yesterday,' I said to Shaina as she fiddled with her phone.

'My sister? Why?'

'I didn't tell her anything. I just asked about you. She doesn't even want me to be in the same universe as you.'

'Then stop trying, Benoy,' she said. 'She loves me too much. And she would never approve of you. She never likes guys around me, Benoy.'

'But why? Why is she so stuck up? It's not as if she has never dated anyone,' I said, frustrated. 'Does she know about the other guys in your life? Like Manoj?'

'Okay, whatever. We are not talking about him.'

'Why not! You dated *him*?'

'I don't want to talk about him. Can you respect that?' she asked. Not wanting to anger her, I stayed silent. 'Manoj is smart and he is really mature. Diya approves of him.'

'I thought we weren't talking about him,' I grumbled, rage coursing through my body.

An awkward silence hung around us.

'Umm, Benoy, I really like you, but we have to stop this,' she said.

'Stop what?'

'Meeting secretly, talking on the phone, your flirting with me. You think it's harmless but it's not,' she explained.

'I would never do anything to harm you. Why would you say that?'

'I can't explain everything to you, but we've got to stop meeting each other. If you ever have to see me, we can catch up in the presence of my sister,' she murmured, her voice low and serious.

'But why?'

'You make me like you, and that's wrong on so many levels that I can't even begin to explain to you,' she said. Every word of hers broke my heart into a million pieces; I could feel it happening in excruciating slow motion.

'I am glad to hear you like me,' I said and forced a smile, wanting to cry.

'My sister doesn't like it and you don't have the slightest idea how my parents would react if they came to know,' she said. 'You only spell trouble for me. I don't like thinking about you, about us.'

'It's enough for me to know that you think about us,' I responded.

'You are so wrong for me,' she said and looked away.

'Then, who's right? Manoj?'

'Maybe he is, maybe he's not,' she answered.

'C'mon. He will be dead in a few years. He is already sixty,' I tried to lighten up; this conversation was only breaking me down.

'He is twenty-six.'

'He looks sixty.'

'It's useless talking to you,' she said. 'I don't even know why I am compelled to talk to you.'

'I think it has something to do with the fact that I'm strikingly good-looking,' I said.

'Whatever.'

I looked at her and she smiled at me shyly. She wouldn't talk much that day; she listened to me and my stories, and would just nod, or look away. I didn't talk about us; it depressed her, and it hurt me to see her like that.

'Are we meeting tomorrow?'

'You want to?' she asked.

'I wouldn't let you go home ever if it were up to me.'

'I will let you know. I will have to ask Mom. She asks too many questions these days. I don't have answers for her like I don't have answers for myself,' she said, looking away from me. I didn't like her talking to me in riddles; she felt distant and cold.

I drove back home, distracted, not sure what to make of what she had said. Her doubts, her apprehensions saddened me, but her obvious consideration for what I felt for her gladdened me; I felt like I was in one of her poems, conflicted yet happy, confused yet clear, sad yet infinitely happy.

Maybe that's what being in love means.

Chapter Twenty-four

We had kept meeting, though we never talked about whether or not we liked each other, or what Diya would think, or whether we should date or not; I was cautious about anything I said to her, scared that I might put her off.

That day, I was waiting near her house; I always parked at a safe distance. It had been drizzling for quite some time now, and I saw her at a distance, running, jumping over puddles, dodging traffic, and by the time she reached my car, she was drenched.

The wet white T-shirt she wore clung to her body and her beautifully carved legs glistened as water droplets streamed down them. A small drop of water trickled down her face and rested on her slightly parted, soft, pink lips.

'Hi,' she said and she pulled out tissues from the box and started rubbing the water off herself.

'Hi,' I said, trying hard not to stare.

She was almost bare. I could see the colour of her skin beneath the wet T-shirt, and I tried hard not to stare. I put the heater on full blast and she thanked me for it.

'Stop staring, Benoy, you're embarrassing me,' she said, still trying to get herself dry. I looked away. The rain pouring outside and the near nakedness of Shaina were just an invitation for me to do something stupid.

'I think I should change,' she said.

'Let's go to my place? I will give you something to wear?' I said.

'*Your* place?' she asked. She was sceptical but there was no other choice; she was still dripping.

'Nice house,' she said as she looked around. A few stray strands of wet hair clung to her face and her neck, small beads of raindrops were still stuck to her face, and her neck and further down. I wanted to be those drops and explore her porcelain-smooth skin. I could not help but stare at her fulsome breasts behind her T-shirt, her flat stomach and her thin waist.

'Can you get me a T-shirt?' she asked.

I nodded. Reluctantly, I left and got her a T-shirt and a pair of shorts. She locked the room behind her and changed. I tried not to imagine her bare and in my room; the thought was delicious and so wrong.

Finally, the door creaked open.

'How do I look?' she asked and struck a pose. The T-shirt ended mid-thigh; it was so long that it hid the shorts beneath it.

'You always look amazing!' I said, my heart aflutter.

'The tee is a little big though,' she joked.

We sat on the couch and ordered pizzas for ourselves. She started to talk and I found it hard to concentrate on her words. I tried not to make it obvious that I was checking her out, which I totally was.

Everything was going *perfect*, when suddenly she came back to the topic.

'This isn't right,' she said. 'I shouldn't be here.'

'Can we not talk about that again?' I begged.

'We can't run away from this conversation, Benoy. I am really fond of you. But—'

'But?'

'Benoy, you and I, this will never be. And you know that. The sooner we understand this, the better,' she said.

She said this casually, not realizing that she was killing me from the inside. Instead of just saying this, she could have just ripped the beating heart of me and handed over to me in my palm.

'I am not particularly in the mood to understand that you try to run away from me at the drop of a hat. It's particularly torturous today, since you're looking totally hot,' I said, almost desperate.

'Fine, then, let's watch a movie? Which movie do you want to watch?'

She went through my collection of DVDs and was disappointed that she could only find mindless action movies—just the kind she hated. Disappointed, she asked me to pick one.

'Let's just watch whatever you want to. I think I have bored you enough by making you watch the movies I do. You deserve a break,' she conceded, and suppressed a smile.

I mindlessly picked one and she slipped it into the DVD player. She tapped a few buttons on the remote and the movie started to play. I was still trapped in her words, words she didn't realize could affect me the way they did. She was always good with words.

'Do you mind?' she said, as she slipped right next to me.

I dimmed the lights and instinctively leaned into her; I put my hand across her shoulder and she didn't brush it off. I wanted to stop the movie and ask her what she meant by what she had said. But I was scared to lose that moment. I wanted to make the most of it. The questions could wait for another time. The movie ended, and right before it did, right before the tearful climax, Shaina and I had kissed.

I *kissed* Shaina.

Chapter Twenty-five

A silence hung around the room as if somebody had died. She looked at me, and I looked at her. I did not know what to say. I had no idea what it meant or where it would lead us. She started crying. What happened later was not what I had in mind; it wasn't planned and it was not why I wanted her to come over.

Quietly, she gathered her things and prepared to leave—she did not say a word. I did not know what to say because I did not know what she felt. I wondered if it was because of the guilt of betraying the trust that her parents had in her.

She disappeared into the room to change back into her clothes; they were still wet.

A little later, she came out. I had no idea who had initiated the kiss. I did not feel sorry about it, but she did.

'I am sorry, Benoy.'

'Sorry? Why? You don't have to be sorry,' I said. She still avoided eye contact; she was still crying.

'I should have never come here. I said this was wrong, didn't I?'

'Why is this wrong? This is *perfect*.'

'This is wrong, Benoy. I don't do this. I don't kiss guys I hardly know.' Her voice was desperate now.

'I didn't mean to kiss you. I'm sorry, I'm really sorry.'

'I know you didn't mean to, Benoy. It's my fault. It's because of me. I kissed you back,' she said and began to leave. 'You don't have to apologize. I led you into believing there was something between us.'

'Can we at least talk about it?'

'There is nothing to talk about. Can I *go*?'

I blocked her way. Her silence and her words, both affected me profoundly.

'I am sorry. I didn't mean to kiss you, but I thought—' I said.

'*Yes, I wanted* to kiss you as well. And that's what's wrong, Benoy. Now, please let me go. I can deal with this myself. Please leave me alone.'

'But, Shaina, I *love* you. I don't see what's wrong in this,' I said, feeling betrayed.

'We don't love each other, Benoy. I don't even know what on earth I am doing here!'

'No, Shaina—' I said, but she was in no mood to listen. *Fuck*.

'Didi was right. I should not have called you. It's my fault, Benoy, seriously.' She came close and talked softly. 'You are not to blame. You are too nice, and I fell for it, even though I shouldn't have. Who wouldn't?'

'But you and I, it seems so right, doesn't it?'

'I don't know. I just don't want this to go any further. I cannot do this. Please don't make it any tougher than it already is, Benoy. Please don't ask any questions. I don't have any answers to give you.'

'Is it Manoj?' I don't know why I asked that.

'I said no questions, Benoy,' she said and left the house.

She was crying as she walked away. I knew that image of her leaving my house would haunt me for a long time to come. I went back to the couch and ran my hands over where she had sat. I could still smell her there. I felt dizzy and terrible.

I wondered where I had gone wrong. I played the last half an hour again in my head. But, even if we kissed, what was the big deal? I loved her, and I told her that. And she only had good things to say about me. *Where have I gone wrong? Do I not deserve her?*

I kept calling her, and she kept rejecting my calls. I sent across a million texts, but she did not reply. Maybe, she was dating Manoj, that old creep. If she were, why couldn't she just tell me that.

I had to take a few vodka shots that day to put me to sleep. As I was falling asleep, I wished I would wake up and it would all be a nasty nightmare.

~

It was not a nightmare; it was happening for real. I woke up the next day, two hours too late and my head hurt. There were missed calls and unread texts from Diya. She wanted to meet. Nothing from Shaina. I called her again. There was no answer. This was real. And it hurt.

Chapter Twenty-six

'What the fuck, Benoy? It's already three!' Diya shouted at me as I walked up to her.

She did not look pleased at all. I was supposed to meet Diya at one in the afternoon in Saket and shop for our internship clothes. She told me there was no one else she could go out with. She had noticed my absence from her life recently. My phone was always busy. I was always out with *friends* and hardly ever available. I had been avoiding her calls; talking to her made me feel guiltier.

Just as I had left my place to meet Diya, I had received a text from Shaina.

Benoy, I need some time alone. I need to figure things out. Please don't text me or call me for the time being.

She could take as much time as she wanted to come and fall right back in love with me. That was what I was concerned about. *Shaina needs some time to think, that's all*, I reminded myself.

'I am sorry, Diya! I got stuck somewhere,' I said.

'You are too busy these days. Where do we go first?'

'Umm, Zara?'

She grabbed my hand and dragged me to the outlet. As she pulled me towards the shop, I wondered if things would have been easier if I had kept Diya in the loop since the very beginning.

'Isn't this like too tight? I look like an elephant in tights.'

'This is what everyone wears these days, Diya,' I said. 'And you look hot. Stop wearing clothes that aunties wear.'

'Whatever.'

'If not for anyone else, you can dress up for Eshaan!' I argued; both of them were doing their internship at BMR Advisors.

'Thank you,' she said, after we were done overhauling her wardrobe.

'What? Thank you? You're my best friend! I can do that for you.'

'Okay, listen, Benoy. I talked to someone from LinkedIn who's studying without a scholarship at LSE. I have inboxed you his mail id. You can ask him any questions that you have,' she told me. I had expressed interest in going to LSE with her, but I hadn't done anything about it yet.

'Diya? That's two years away. Why would I need to talk to him *now*?'

'I just felt that you desperately wanted to go,' she said sadly.

'Aw! I really do. Okay, you know what, I have already talked to Dad about it and he will ask people around.'

'You did?' she asked and smiled.

'Yes. I did. I know you will fail your exams there without me. I know how much you need me!' I said, and hugged her.

Hungry and tired, we went to Khan Market to have lunch. I did not say much on the way; I was tired since I had not slept the night before. I toyed with the idea of telling her about Shaina; it seemed like the only option.

As I parked my car, my phone beeped. It was a text from Shaina.

Benoy, I am sorry. We can't be in touch any more. Please don't call or text me. Please understand. This is my last text. Take care. Best of luck in life. I am sorry.

As we went about choosing a place, my head hurt. My hands trembled and I wanted to call her. My stomach felt strange and it seemed I was falling sick.

'What happened?' Diya asked. 'You seem strange. Is everything okay?'

I nodded.

We sat down to eat and I was yet to say anything. She kept asking but I could not form the sentences in my head. I was dazed. I read Shaina's message repeatedly. Finally, I gathered some courage and spoke up. I needed somebody I could talk to regarding Shaina.

'Umm, Diya, I need to tell you something.'

'Tell me?'

'Promise me you won't freak out and will first listen to everything I say.'

'Sure.'

I started to narrate everything that had happened between Shaina and me in the past few weeks. She sat motionless as I told her everything, leaving nothing out. I tried to convince her that Shaina meant the world to me and that this was not any fling, and that I was not a fling sort of a guy; her face gave nothing away, and I didn't know if she believed me. I showed her the text Shaina had just sent me. As she finished reading it, tears rolled down her cheeks. She said *nothing*. She just looked away like her sister always did whenever she had to smile. Or cry.

'Are you okay?'

'I need some time alone.'

'I can explain things, Diya.'

'Just fuck off, Benoy,' she said, got up and stormed off.

I ran after her, trying to calm her, but she wouldn't listen. I followed her to the metro station. She kept crying silently even as she boarded the metro.

'But at least say *something*!' I said, as she disappeared inside the metro.

Twice in two days, I had seen people I loved truly cry and walk all over me and away. *They will come back*, I told myself. I was sure that they would be sorry some day. Diya would beg me to accompany her to LSE. And Shaina would ask me to kiss her again.

Everything will be all right, I said to myself.

~

I drove back home with nothing to look forward to. I checked my phone repeatedly. No texts. No missed calls. I started to call both the sisters incessantly, hoping to make them understand.

Diya was not replying to my messages. But she finally answered my call.

'At least say something, Diya,' I said. 'I said I'm sorry.'

'There is nothing to say, Benoy.'

'I didn't mean to hide it. But you were so—'

'Let it be. I don't want any explanations,' she grumbled.

'But—'

'Benoy, just don't call me. I need to talk to my sister. I will get back to you.'

'But—'

'Don't call me unless I do. I don't want you anywhere near me,' she said and cut the line. I did not want her to fight with Shaina because of me, but clearly, it was going to happen. Hours passed by, I did not hear a single word from either of them. I was nervous and it was almost two when Diya finally called me—her voice stern, her words straightforward.

'Hi, Benoy.'

'Hi, Diya. Look, I am sorry . . . but—'

'You don't have to be. I told you I love my sister way too much and I would never let anything happen to her,' she said.

'I would—'

'Just listen, Benoy. I do not know what you feel for my sister. And I really don't know what she feels for you. I talked to her about it and she is not sure about you. It's better that you two don't talk,' she said, very coldly. 'I hope you listen this time.' It reminded me of the day when she first talked to me—cold, heartless, ruthless.

'At least let me talk to her once.'

'Benoy? There is something else, too, that you need to know.'

'What is it?' I asked.

'Shaina has been seeing a guy for the last two years.'

'*What?* She is seeing someone? Who? Manoj?'

'Yes.'

'But she never told me about that!' I protested.

'She never told me either, Benoy,' she snapped. 'She told Manoj about you and they broke up.'

'So that's good, right, Diya? I really like your sister. I really do, trust me.'

'NOTHING IS RIGHT, BENOY!' she shouted. 'Manoj came with his parents to our place. He told my parents everything about their two-year-old relationship. Dad thrashed Shaina till she almost passed out. I was there, Mom was there. Dad even accused me of being a part of it. It was Manoj who stopped Dad and told him that he wanted to marry Shaina.'

'What did your parents say?' I asked, my heart thumping in my chest.

'They like him. I told you what they are like, Benoy. They are already fixing dates for her engagement. They don't want people to know that Shaina was in a relationship. You have no idea how my relatives will react,' she said.

'*What?* How can they do this? I need to talk to Shaina. Please understand, Diya. I really need to talk to her. Can I please do that?' I begged.

'Shaina is sitting right next to me and she doesn't want to talk to you,' Diya explained.

Every word, every sentence felt like death, permanent

and damaging. I shuddered to think what Shaina had gone through for me.

'But what do I do now?' I asked her.

'I don't know. That's for you to handle, Benoy. Please leave us alone and go away. That's the least you can do. Please don't screw us up more,' she said, her voice cracking.

'Can I at least talk to her?' I begged.

'No, BENOY! You can't!' she growled. 'Don't make it worse for Shaina and me. Manoj is a nice guy and he loves her. Please leave us ALONE! And don't ever call here again.'

Silence.

She had disconnected the call. All was lost. There was no silver lining; it wasn't one of Shaina's poems; I wasn't getting a second chance; I wasn't the magical puppy with broken legs, but with glittery wings. My fairy tale had hit a road block, a dead end; the fondness, the softness of her touch, the warm hugs, the stolen glances—all of it was a lie, a mirage, a trick to deceive me. I started writing, hoping to put together in words what I felt, like Shaina used to, and I wrote it down. It didn't make me feel any better.

> I didn't know what went wrong, what made her walk
> away.
> I tried to figure out, but nothing she would say,
> For my questions pestered her, my tears made her
> embarrassed.
> I never wanted to be a priority, but a little love was all
> I expected.
>
> I still kept giving, giving, day in and out.
> But all went in vain, when all she beheld were doubts.

Doubts of an uncertain tomorrow, so she told me, 'I have to go.'

My dreams, my wishes, my love were shattered in a single blow.

I stood by the balcony, looking into the thin air.

I clung on to her picture, crying silently so that no one saw.
All I begged of my fate, was a sight of her.

Occupied with things important, she had moved on well in life.
It was never tough for her, for I was another man by her side.
She thought I must be over her by then; least was she aware that I died each day.

I moved out, I had forgotten how it felt being loved.
I sought a place to pour my heart out, I looked below and above.
When saw no place to confine, saw no place to cry my heart out,
I kept walking towards a dead end, against the fate I had enough fought.
I reached the valley, stood there high, saw down the abyss and looked behind.
When saw no one who would call me back, I let my body be taken down by the wind.

They located my body amidst the woods, with a note in my hand clutched tight.
And a picture of her in my hand.

It read, 'I will love you till I die,
don't let her know of my death,
She might live life in guilt.
Just tell her I went to a place afar,
And though I loved her still.'

I stood there while they laid my corpse; a kid asked me
   who he was
I told him 'a part of me'.

Chapter Twenty-seven

My internship had started and it had been two days since I had been going to the office. Since I literally owned the place, I really had nothing to do, and I remembered the time Diya had asked me to take the internship seriously, but I had no motivation to do so now. My days were a gigantic mess, cluttered with thoughts and memories of Shaina and Diya, all of them painful.

I sat in my seat and could not decide whether to call up Dad or Shaina, and while Shaina, I knew, would not ever pick up my call, Dad would be dying to receive my call. I called up Dad. It felt somewhat stupid to explain what had happened.

'Hello?' I said.

'Hi, Benoy, everything going fine in office?'

'Yes, yes. I needed to talk to you about something else.'

'Tell me.'

'I was wondering if I could come to your office.'

He said he would be in my office in another two hours or so. As I leaned back into my chair, I wondered how the conversation would go.

'I know we haven't talked in the last two decades, but I really love this girl and it's all screwed up and I want you to straighten this out.'

Or,

'The girl I really like is kind of getting engaged, so can you please talk to her parents and ask her to cancel it because I am in love with her. The girl? Yeah, she's not sure about me. I think she doesn't think I'm worth ending her two-year-long relationship or fighting with her parents.'

There was a knock on the door. It had not even been an hour and I saw Dad standing outside looking like a high-profile lawyer from a sitcom in his sharply cut suit and shiny black shoes. Not a sidekick, but the *main guy*. I was proud of him. The anger I had for him had slowly melted away after I had seen the contents of the envelope, and though I hadn't talked to him about it, I was sure he knew I had forgiven him.

'Hey,' he said and pulled up a chair. 'How do you find *your* new office?'

'It's a little more than I deserve,' I said.

'So? What did you want to talk to me about?' he asked.

'Umm. There is this girl . . .'

'Shaina?'

'How do you know?' I asked. 'Oh right. You know everything about me. What else do you know? Did you tap my phones? Did you tap hers?'

'Should I have tapped hers?' he asked, leaning forward, a twinkle in his eyes, like he was about to snap his fingers and it would be done, no questions asked. God! He was cool.

'No, it's fine,' I said.

Then I started speaking, and he hung on to every word as I narrated the entire story. Dad nodded his head from time to time and asked questions about Shaina and Diya, almost like making a timeline of events in his head.

'So? You want me to talk to their parents? I can do that,' he said. 'She doesn't have to get engaged right now. It's too early for her.'

'But what would you say?' I asked.

'I will say whatever you want me to say,' he answered.

'I will let you know,' I murmured. 'All of this is so confusing. I don't even know if Shaina wants me.'

'Of course she wants you. Who wouldn't want my son? Look at you. You're handsome and intelligent. I don't think she can do better than you. It will be okay,' he assured me.

I smiled at him. He talked to me about work and office and told me that I could take as much time as I wanted to settle down.

'I have a really boring meeting with the lawyers. Can I see you later?' he asked.

'Yeah, sure. I will be right here, doing nothing,' I said.

'Cheer up, Benoy. It will be okay. She will come running after you!' he said and winked. He left for the meeting.

Later that evening, I lost it and broke down. The hurt was almost physical and I didn't know what I had to do to make it all go away. My head hurt, and I felt like dying, like, literally dying. I thought of drinking myself to sleep but it would come back the next day. This loss was permanent; it was never going away. I panicked. Thinking of Manoj and Shaina made me want to kill somebody.

I called up Dad and asked him if he could call Shaina's father and do something about the situation.

Chapter Twenty-eight

I waited for Dad to call me back. It had been an hour since I had texted him the number. The doorbell rang. It was Dad standing outside, his shoulders drooping, his eyes overflowing with despair, and I knew he had nothing but bad news.

Dad told me that Shaina had known Manoj for five years, and they had been in a relationship for two years. Shaina had told him that they were in love, and both their families were happy with the decision they had made. She had added that she never loved me, and wanted me to stay away from her.

Her parents asked Dad and his disgraceful son, me, to never call anyone in their family again; they even threatened to file a police complaint against my dad and me. They told him how uncultured I was. They told him that I had not been brought up well because I had grown up in a broken family. They called Dad names and told him that he had been a bad father and a damaging influence on me. They called him vile and uncouth. I felt sorry for Dad; he didn't need to bear the assault for my mistakes.

'I'm sorry, Dad,' I said. 'I didn't know they would say so much.'

'You want me to stay. We can drink it away if you want to.'

I felt good about him being the kind of *cool dad* that everyone wants, but I knew even drinking wouldn't solve this.

'I will be fine. But thank you so much, Dad.'

'I am sorry I couldn't make a difference.'

'You did what you could do,' I said.

We talked for twenty more minutes. I asked a few more questions and the more I got to know, the more my heart broke. He left, even though he really wanted to stay. But I wanted some time alone.

What was she thinking? One last fling? The questions kept haunting me all night and in a fit of anger and depression, I called up Shaina, but her phone was still switched off.

Frustrated, I called up Diya. It was probably the fifteenth call that she answered and by this time, I was on the verge of breaking down again.

'Diya,' I said, crying. Almost howling.

'Benoy?' she said. 'Are you okay?'

'Umm . . .'

'Are you okay, Benoy?'

'Should I be okay?'

'But?'

I disconnected the line.

She called back almost immediately. I disconnected the line once again. I needed someone to talk to, not someone I would have to explain everything to. But she kept calling over and over again.

'Benoy, can we talk, please?'

'There is nothing to talk about. You got what you wanted. You wanted me to stay away from her, and see, I am nowhere near her! She doesn't even want me near here!'

'Benoy, I really had no idea about how you felt for her.'

'You DIDN'T? Didn't I tell you that day like a million times over that I *love* her? Didn't I? Didn't I send you over a hundred texts saying the same thing?'

'But—'

'What but?'

'I wasn't sure! You can't blame me for it. Both of you didn't tell me ANYTHING! HOW WAS I SUPPOSED TO KNOW, BENOY!' she shouted.

'You know, just fuck off. You and your sister, both of you. I don't need you guys! Just GO AWAY!' I said and disconnected the line.

She called again and I disconnected the line. She was not helping. I could have done without her. But her incessant calling made me pick up the phone again. It was irritating.

'Benoy, I am sorry. At least FUCKING LISTEN TO ME. I didn't know what to do with you guys. Both of you were lying to me! BOTH OF YOU! And how was I to know what you felt for my sister was genuine?'

'Well, now you know.'

I cut the line and lay back on the couch with both my hands on my head. I just wanted to ask Shaina if she was so sure about Manoj, why did she encourage me and let me fall in love with her? As I flicked through the pictures of Shaina and me—the two of us smiling—I knew it was real, that both of us felt it and it wasn't just in my head. I knew I was more than a friend.

I was not ready to accept that the best days of my life were a lie. I loved her. And I would keep doing so. For me, it was real, and it would always be.

Chapter Twenty-nine

It was just a crush, get over it!
I lost count of how many times I said this to myself and forcefully smiled. I hoped the next moment would be better, but it just remained the same. I did not want to talk to anyone. Not Diya, not Shaina and not anyone else. I tried hard to be normal. There were days when I totally locked myself in, spent hours crying, but I knew that it was not a solution, so I tried to be normal with everyone. Deb and Avantika had been going through the best phase in their lives. They were engaged now, their families knew and they didn't have to sneak around to be together.

On the other hand, Shaina had called me a rich, irresponsible brat, who was obsessive, had nothing to do and needed to be reined in.

It was eight in the evening and everyone in the office had left when Dad walked into my office.

'Are you still working?' he asked as he came in.

'Umm . . . yes,' I said.

Over the last few days, I had realized the only way I could keep that beautiful *fucking* face out of my mind was by staying in office. I would call her sometimes, from the office lines which were one-way calling, so I could call her, hear her say '*Hello*' over and over again and keep the phone down.

'Is something wrong?' he asked.

'No, what could be wrong?'

'Benoy, it really doesn't have to end like this,' he said. 'I'm not good with women or relationships, but I think she was pressurized to say what she did.'

'Dad, I called her up so many times since that day but she told me to stay away. She doesn't even reply to my texts. She has even changed her number twice,' I said.

'Benoy, you can't just expect her to end her two-year-long relationship with a guy just because she spent three weeks with you. I now know the kind of community she belongs to. It wouldn't take seconds for people to know that she dated somebody and then broke the engagement. It's a little too much to ask for,' he explained. 'Having said that, I don't think she deserves what's happening to her.'

'I hate her family,' I said.

'Not more than me, son. So, not leaving office any time soon?' he asked.

'In just a little while.'

He left and I put my head down on the table. I thought the days would get easier as they passed. I hoped I would start hating Shaina for what she had said about me, and

I really thought I would get over it, but it was far from it and I hated it. I leaned back on the chair and looked at the ceiling. I could see her, smiling at me, laughing at me for being such a fool to think that a girl like her would ever love me.

Then there was a knock on the door. It was Deb, and Avantika followed closely behind.

'Hey,' Deb said, 'what's up, man?'

'What the fuck are you doing here?' I asked. 'Dad asked you to come over, didn't he? I am fine, guys. You didn't have to come.'

'Oh, fuck off, Benoy,' Deb barked. 'No one cares about you. We need to use your house.'

'Is it?' I asked, sceptical.

'We actually had to go out, but then the club has no reservations available today, and we don't want to waste the night,' Avantika explained.

'Let me talk to Dad. He will get you in some club, I am sure!'

'Don't do that! It will look so bad on us. I really don't want that,' Avantika pleaded and made a cute face.

Pretty girls always win arguments. We sat in my car and we left for my place. I tried to be normal; I laughed with them and tried to be as funny as I could because I did not want anyone to worry too much about me; it wasn't worth it. They asked if things were fine and I nodded. Things were indeed fine; it just felt a little incomplete, like I had been robbed of something.

'*Oye*, Benoy. A friend of Avantika is coming over, too,' he said. 'You wouldn't mind, right?'

'Oh please! Don't tell me you are setting me up with somebody. I really don't need this right now.'

'We are not trying to set you up,' Deb said.

'Fuck off,' I barked.

Avantika continued, 'We just told her that you've been single for long and you are extremely nice. And then, she wanted to meet you! Honest. She saw you on Facebook. It's not really our fault.'

'But why, Avantika? I am all right! You don't need to do all this.'

'Oh, c'mon. Don't be such a prick. Give her a chance at least,' she said. 'Maybe you will like her!'

'You didn't have to do this. I am sorry, but I think she will be very bored today. She will have the worst day of her life today and she will hate the two of you for it,' I said.

'Ohh, c'mon! Two drinks down your throat and you will tie her to your bed!' Avantika said. 'We all know you well.'

'Maybe *not*,' I said.

We reached my place and waited for her to turn up. Avantika got busy in arranging the house, putting things where they should have been, while Deb and I got ourselves a couple of beers.

'So, it was your idea? Why don't you get it, man? I don't even know what I will say to this girl. This is so screwed up,' I ranted.

'I swear it was Avantika's idea. She still thinks that you will get over it. And this was another one of your flings.'

'And you know it's not?'

'I don't know what it was, but it was certainly not a fling for you. Girls as pretty and smart as her . . . you don't ever find them again,' he said in hushed tones. I was glad he understood.

Soon the bell rang and Avantika went to get it; I was already bored and Deb asked me to stop rolling my eyes. A girl dressed in hideous loose clothes and a pair of spectacles straight out of hell walked in.

'Hi, Benoy,' she said.

'Diya? What on earth are *you* doing here?' I asked, shocked.

'I came to see you,' she said.

'Ummm . . . I should be so angry right now,' I said. 'Ideally I should kill you.'

'Oh bullshit. I know you can never be pissed at me for long,' she quipped. We hugged each other. 'I missed you, Benoy.'

'I missed you more,' I said, 'even though you're one of the evil sisters who totally wrecked my life.'

'At least I am the pretty one!' she said.

We laughed and then we cried.

'I didn't think I would miss you so much!' she said.

'I missed you more!' I said. 'Trust me. I hated you more than I missed you, but I did miss you a lot.'

We all had a little laugh. The pizza Avantika had ordered suddenly tasted better.

'So,' Avantika asked Diya, 'Benoy isn't all that bad, is he?'

'Now, don't embarrass me. I really didn't mean any harm. She is my sister after all. Moreover, I didn't think he was bad. I just thought he was not right for my sister.'

'We don't blame you,' Deb said. 'But what's with your sister? No offence though! I really don't buy that Benoy stalked her.'

'I am sure she has a reason for whatever she said that day,' I said.

'Oho?' Avantika butted in. 'After all this, still defending her, Benoy? You're so gone, man.'

'I don't mind being in love with her, Avantika.'

'I am sorry, Benoy,' Diya said again.

'It's okay, Diya. I screwed up. There's nothing you could have done.'

'Benoy?' Deb asked me. 'Don't you want to at least ask what was going through Shaina's head? What was she thinking?'

'I don't want to complicate her life. And really, she never explicitly said that she loved me, so it's fine. I am sure her guy is nice and she will be happy with him. I think he's ugly as shit, but then it's okay. I also wish he gets run over by a truck.'

'Or gets stuck inside heavy machinery and gets torn apart!' Deb said, excitedly.

'Or drowns!' Avantika added. 'I am sure your dad can manage this.'

'I'm sure he can,' Diya said. 'I just heard he bought half of the United States and a third of Great Britain. Is that right?'

'Ha ha, very funny,' I retorted. 'But is she happy with Manoj?' I had not seen her update her blog or upload pictures of her sketches; I wondered if her parents had let the steam off her a little bit.

'Benoy, the only reason why Manoj told his parents was because Shaina told him about you. He was just jealous and furious and he felt cheated,' Diya said.

'But Shaina agreed to the engagement, right?' I asked.

'She should have been happy that her boyfriend of two years finally told her parents, but all she has done is cry,' Diya explained.

'It's okay for him to be possessive. Maybe he panicked. But I am sure she loves him,' I said.

Deb interrupted and said, 'I am sure it was Manoj who had put the words into Shaina's mouth. That bastard.'

'That could be true. I know my sister and she is not like that. She cannot be this rude,' she said. 'And, Benoy, even if Shaina loves you, she won't tell you; she can't. My parents are already not talking to her. Can you even imagine what would happen?'

'So what now? We just sit here and do nothing?' Avantika asked.

'Yes, that's what we are going to do. Nothing is going to come out of this discussion. This is stupid,' I said. 'Don't give me hope because there isn't any.'

'Benoy,' Diya said, 'the only reason why I came here was because I had started believing in you. And I really think that if there is anybody who should be with her, it's you. Don't let me down now.'

'That's sweet of you, but I don't know what she feels for me, Diya. For all you know, she hates me now,' I said.

'We will see,' she said and smiled at me.

I had reasons to get drunk that night.

Diya was confident that there was some place in Shaina's heart for me. That was reason enough for me to be happy. I had to make a physical effort to stop myself from dreaming and thinking about the day when Shaina and I would be together again. I felt extremely cheesy, when I automatically replaced the imaginary guy (Manoj!) in the engagement, and I could see Shaina and me exchanging rings and smiling at each other, kissing each other. The daydream sequence kicked all my other daydreams' asses pretty bad!

I talked a lot about Shaina that night; the play of her name, *Shaina*, on my lips felt like heaven.

Chapter Thirty

There was good news in the air and a spring in my step. There was something to cheer about. Though Shaina was still ridiculously unattainable, I felt good, thinking that her own sister and my best friend had faith in me. I went to the office that day thinking about her, as I always did, but I wasn't depressed any more.

I had been avoiding Eshaan's calls for quite some time now. I called him up.

'Hi, what's up? They didn't make you the CFO yet?' I asked Eshaan.

'They are still deciding on it,' he answered. 'How are you, Benoy? You don't answer your phone any more, Benoy?'

'Things weren't so good for the last few days.'

'Diya told me about your problems with Shaina. It will be okay. If you need anything, just give me a call.'

'Fingers crossed! And tell me, how's office? How's the crowd?' I asked.

153

'We are the youngest here, Benoy,' he said.

'Haven't you started hitting on Diya yet? You have a shot with her, Eshaan,' I said.

'I don't know! I have heard what her parents are like and I don't want to get into that. And I don't think she even likes me.'

'Have you tried telling her that you like her?'

'I don't like her!' he said. 'She is cute. But there is nothing of that sort between us, Benoy.'

'But you two are so similar! You can spend years talking about important economic stuff. That's so your thing. There is no reason why you shouldn't be together,' I suggested. 'You two are *made* for each other. Don't ruin it!'

We talked for another twenty-odd minutes and he returned to his work, and I kept thinking about how desperately I wanted the two of them to be together. They were so meant to be.

~

Diya and I had been planning this for long now.

In the past few days, Diya had often mentioned me in her conversations with Shaina to elicit reactions, but Shaina asked Diya not to talk about me any more.

I waited in that coffee shop for Shaina to turn up. It was supposed to be a sister's day out. That is what at least Diya *told* Shaina. It had been forty minutes since I had been waiting and looking in the mirror every five seconds to check whether I looked all right. My heart was beating as if tiny earthquakes were hitting it periodically.

She walked in, and she looked as gorgeous as she always did. She started looking for her sister, and instead found me.

'Hey,' I said; almost immediately, her expression changed to one of horror and surprise. She did not look pleased at all; my heart sank.

'Benoy? What—'

'Can we talk? Before you say anything?'

Before I could even get up, she stormed off, banging the door as she left. I followed her outside the coffee shop; she was waving at autorickshaws.

'What? Benoy, I don't want to talk to you. Is that too hard to understand?'

'Yes, it is and this is driving me crazy. All I want from you is the answers to a few questions and I will not bother you ever again!'

'Are you sure?' she said. 'Because once I sort this out with you, I don't want to have anything to do with you. Are we clear about this?'

She was cold and heartless, and broke my heart into further smaller pieces with every word she said.

'Can we just go inside?' I begged her.

We didn't order anything. The waiter hovered near us and Shaina swatted him away.

'Why?' I asked her.

'I am not the person you want to be with. Please just forget it like any other fling of yours. It was a mistake, Benoy, and you know that.'

'It wasn't a mistake. I had never been surer about anything. And I didn't even know about Manoj. You didn't think it was important for me to know?'

'I didn't want to. And it was a mistake telling you anything. I did not want this. He forgave me once; he will not do that again. I really need to go.' Her voice was calm, frosty.

'What if this is meant to be and not what you have with Manoj?'

'You hardly know me, Benoy. Manoj and I have known each other for five years now. We are in love. He is right for me. Moreover, my parents are involved now. It's too late for everything.'

I looked for signs that might tell me that she was lying. She looked straight at me with those big, brown eyes, and no matter how hard I stared, I didn't see compassion or empathy for what I was going through.

'I don't want to lose him,' she declared.

'So you regret whatever happened between us?' I asked her.

'Yes, I do. I wish nothing had happened. I wish I could undo everything. I need to go, Benoy,' she said, looking nervously at her phone.

'You can't just go like that,' I begged, now desperate.

'I don't have to answer everything. And please, I don't want to hear from you ever again.'

She got up from her seat and picked up her handbag to leave.

'Shaina,' I said, 'at all the times I said to you that I loved you, I had been truer than I had ever been in my entire life.'

'I'm really sorry,' she said and left, running out of the door of the cafe, on to the street and into an autorickshaw. I thought I saw her crying.

I kept sitting in the cafe and waited for Diya. I felt stupid. I was twenty and I was crying my heart out for a girl when most guys looked for an easy lay, someone good in bed, someone *easy* to bed.

Diya and I sat there and she said everything that could have made me feel better, but nothing worked.

'There is no point in this, Benoy,' Diya said. 'I wish I could do something for you. You will find many nice girls, Benoy. Just—'

'I am not looking for anyone else. And I don't care about what she said or what she did, I still love her. I will be okay, Diya.'

'I don't know what to say. But I think my sister missed out on the *best* guy ever. I can't believe I couldn't help you out,' she said apologetically.

'Don't be hard on yourself,' I said and she hugged me.

I dropped her home, and after half an hour of absent-minded driving, I reached Dad's office. The entire office was empty and the only lights on were in his cabin at the corner of the floor. It was Saturday night after all. He had nowhere to go to and neither did I.

'Still working?' I said as I got inside. 'Hmm. The whole office is empty.'

'Oh, not really!' he said and flipped the laptop down.

'I have nothing to do. Everyone out there has someone to go back home to. This is home for me,' he said. 'So, what happened today?'

'Shaina made it very clear that she wanted to be with him. And she doesn't want to be around me.'

'And what did you say?'

'I had nothing to say! What could I have? I literally had to beg her to talk to me. As much as I love her, it was really, you know, humiliating.'

'Benoy? Did your mom ever tell you how I got her?'

'We never really talked about the two of you,' I said.

'Hmm. I guessed that,' he said and started to narrate. 'I saw her at the community Durga Puja. My grandparents approached your mother's parents with the proposal and they rejected it outright. I was into business and no one appreciated that. Everyone wanted an engineer or a government servant.

'I wasn't even a graduate while your mother was already teaching in a college. I started stalking your mom and she even complained to my parents but I was obstinate. I really wanted her. Slowly, my business grew and her parents relented. But even before they agreed, I knew she was in love with me.'

'That's quite a story,' I said.

'But, it didn't work out as I wanted it to. Work had become such an obsession for me. I worked day and night even after I married your mom. I thought I was doing all this for the two of you,' he said and added after a pregnant pause, 'but I was just doing it for myself.'

'Mom told me that.'

'I have rued everything that I have ever done since. Except your mother's fading days. I tried convincing her to let me talk to you, but she never agreed. She never wanted me near you. She said I had made you cry enough already.'

'I don't remember,' I said.

'You were small then, and you never used to see me for months on end. I was like a total stranger to you. You used to be fonder of Deb's dad than me,' he said. 'Anyway, what do you know about this guy Manoj? I am not too convinced about him!'

'As in? I know nothing about him,' I said. 'What do you plan to do? Please don't screw it up more than it already is!'

'Give me a few days, I will find out everything there is to know about him—where he works, his vices, loans, anything. Let's have him followed for a few days and find something wrong about him. We make conditions so bad for him that he breaks up with her. Whatever works,' Dad said.

'You're scaring me now. How often have you done this?'

'Not very often.' He laughed. He looked wicked with his salt-and-pepper slick hair, his black suit and tie, the British accent and that evil grin on his face.

'I don't think we should do it. She told me that she loves him. Why deprive her of that?'

'What if that guy is not good? There is no harm in getting to know him better. Okay, Benoy, we will do nothing, just pull some information about him and see what comes out,' he assured me. 'If you love Shaina that much, don't you want to know about the guy she will spend her life with?'

It seemed like he already knew that something was wrong with her guy. Then, I thought, *What the hell, let me go through with this*. I crossed my fingers and wished Manoj had a murky history. Old beaten girlfriends, drug abuse, sex offences, anything!

Dad and I went to dinner that night. It was nice, actually. We talked about Mom, and about the times that we were a family. Despite his screw-ups on the family front, he was pretty darn awesome. He had amazing stories to tell and I could see why Mom fell for him. He was charming and suddenly I missed him for not being around all these years. It would have been nice to have a cool dad.

Maybe I would have been a better guy had my dad been around.

'I loved your mom,' he said. 'I would change everything if I had to live my life again. I would give up everything to be with you and your mother. That is all that matters to me. And now, you are all that matters to me.'

I choked on my tears but I just smiled. It is great to have a family. I felt sorry for my dad that he could no longer tell my mother that he loved her. He still missed her. I missed her, too.

I slept soundly that night.

I wished Manoj was a serial killer. A sex offender would work fine too.

Chapter Thirty-one

'Incredible!' Eshaan said.

He looked around with his mouth wide open enough for an elephant to pass through; Diya clutched at his hand. Eshaan had asked Diya out, but she had promptly turned him down, telling him that she needed to get to LSE first, relationships could come later; they were good friends though.

'I said the same thing when I saw this place for the first time,' I said, referring to Dad's house.

I had shifted there. Over the last few weeks, Dad's driver would pick up and drop me home. Slowly, I began staying at Dad's place for a few nights in a row because we worked late. It had started being fun so I had decided to move in with Dad. It was an incredible house after all! At the last count, the mansion had five floors, uncountable bedrooms, a dozen conference rooms, two mini theatres and five gaming consoles. It seemed like he was planning to lure me into his house. And it worked.

I had started to find peace in his company. He used to talk about all the things he had done and achieved in the course of his life, and all the places he had been to, all the people he had met with . . . it was all quite inspiring. The past few days brought me closer to Dad. I felt a connection. He was always there when I needed someone, he listened to me when I complained, and he never judged me. I had genuinely started liking him.

'So are you going to live here?' Diya asked.

'I think so.'

'But why?' Eshaan said, 'I thought you always liked to live alone.'

'Not any more it seems.'

'It seems so long since we have sat and talked,' Diya said as Eshaan went ahead and explored the house more.

'I know.'

'Have you been avoiding me?'

'No, Diya! Why would I avoid you?'

'Maybe, I remind you of her.'

'You do. But you also remind me of college and our shitty professors. And, really, I do not mind even if you do remind me of her. I only smile when I think of her.'

'You know how cheesy you sound when you say these things, right? If you were saying this for someone else other than my sister, I am sure I would have puked,' she jested.

'I can't help it, Diya. Even if she is not with me, I feel her around. And that's what keeps me happy.'

'I really had never thought that I would see someone *so* much in love. I used to hear stories like this, but I never thought it would happen so close to me. And I feel so sorry to have misjudged you. You have no idea how bad I feel,' she said.

'I have told you before and I am telling you now. Stop blaming yourself,' I scolded her.

'I am so angry at my sister! I don't know why she just doesn't stand up to Dad and say she loves you!' she said, exasperated. 'Manoj isn't half as good as you are. He doesn't even know how to talk. He sits amongst us and stays shut. I don't know what my sister sees in him!'

'I am sure he keeps her happy,' I said.

'I have just seen her cry. He doesn't even let her meet her friends. It's so frustrating.'

'That's expected. She cheated on him; it's okay to be a little possessive,' I said.

'A little? He doesn't even let her meet her female friends! A few days back, she had put up a picture of hers in a skirt and he called her a *prostitute*! Imagine that! Who does that? They are not even engaged yet.'

'Did she tell you that? He actually called her that?' I asked.

'I read their messages,' she said. 'He apologized, but he made her delete all the pictures! And blocked every guy friend of hers.'

'Is he a caveman?' If I were dating Shaina, I would have wanted to show off to the world that I was dating the cutest girl ever. Why would I ever *block* people?

'So what does Shaina say about this?' I asked and she shook her head. 'But why? Today he's blocking people, tomorrow he will be hitting her.'

'She's a little too deep into this. I don't think she has the strength to fight Dad any more. And the day she came back after meeting you, she cried the entire night,' she said. 'I am so worried about her.'

Eshaan came back all excited, and narrated an inventory of items the house had, most of which I had no idea about.

'You can shift in with me,' I offered Eshaan.

'Are you crazy? I would never leave this house!' he shot back.

~

Manoj had proved to be squeaky clean as per my dad, but then these were things that could not be verified. If Shaina chose to be with someone who was crazy possessive about her, then who was I to stop her?

I was just glad that college was reopening the next day and I hoped Diya would put me on an unrelenting schedule of studies and assignments and fuck-boring classes. I looked forward to the busy life. And hoped it would cure me a little. However, I had figured that would never happen.

I had lost all hope.

Chapter Thirty-two

'C'mon, Benoy, that girl is hot,' Diya said.

She pointed out someone in our Career Launcher class. I had noticed her, too. Yes, she was cute. However, my definition of being cute had changed since I met Shaina. For me, she was the only cute person in the world and she defined the word for me, and she defined a lot of other words like love and forever and happiness and heartbreak and what not.

'We're just on the third question! Let's concentrate,' I said.

We had attended three classes and all she could do was point out girls I could possibly hit on. This was the English class, so I could still tolerate her, but she was even doing it in the mathematics class, and it was irritating.

'No, Diya, I liked no one!'

'Are you sure?'

'Yes, I am sure! And stop worrying about me so much. You can see that I am fine now. I am over her.'

'Okay, I am getting late. I should go now,' she said. Manoj's parents were coming over to her place that day; it was a pre-engagement ritual and Diya was already late for it. I was sure that by that time Shaina would have already got ready in some elegant-looking ethnic wear. Diya told me Shaina had decided on a bright red sari.

'Do you want me to drop you?'

'No, I will be fine. Will you be okay?' she asked.

'I will be fine. Now *go*! Or you will be late. I can't believe she's getting engaged today. Wish her luck.'

'She's not getting engaged today. We are just calling pandits over and they will choose an auspicious date within the next month,' she clarified.

'Same thing,' I answered.

I hugged her and saw her off.

This function was just the beginning of it; in a few days she would get engaged, and then maybe get married after a year or two; I was screwed. Diya had tried convincing her parents against getting Shaina engaged so soon, but her parents did not budge. They felt their daughter had disgraced them and they wanted to arrive at an engagement date sooner than soon. They came from a very conservative community and the news of a girl's affair travelled far and wide in a matter of days. A roka, or a formal union like an engagement, was the only way they could have stopped people from talking dirty about their daughter. Shaina had not said anything.

I drove my way back home, knowing well that Dad must have made an elaborate plan to straighten out my mood. Dad, too, had made some major changes. He had sold off some of his businesses so that he had more time to spend with me. A little late in the day, but I guessed he did not want to screw up the second time around.

We had started drinking together, and what is better to soothe broken relationships than a couple of beers every day? We drank like tankers that day. Usually Dad stopped me after a few beers, but that day, he just let me drink till I knocked myself out.

Till the time I hadn't passed out, I had to try hard to keep back my tears every time I imagined Shaina in her *bright red*, exquisite ethnic wear, in a ceremony with someone else.

I knew the pain would never go.

Chapter Thirty-three

The next day, my head hurt; I found myself tucked inside a blanket on the couch where I must have passed out the night before. My phone had a few missed calls and I looked around to see if my dad was there. He was not. *He is probably sleeping*, I thought. I got up groggily and brushed my teeth. I came back and picked up my cell phone.

Within ten seconds, I was wide awake and staring at the screen; it was like someone had punched me in the stomach. There were thirteen missed calls from Shaina and two texts asking me to call her as soon as possible.

My heart raced, and I daydreamed that she had called it off and had run away from her home, or maybe she had managed to convince her parents. My hands trembled as I made that call, hoping to find a frantic and apologetic Shaina on the other side, dying to get back with me. Blood rushed through my veins, my face flushed and felt warm as I could not hold back my excitement. I paced around the room and hoped for good news on the other side of the phone. I was hopeful.

The first call. No answer. *Probably Shaina is busy explaining to everybody why she wants to call it off.*

The second call. No answer. *Probably Diya is telling her how right she is in her decision.*

The third call. No answer. *Probably they are discussing how to tackle me and how to tell me that they are sorry.*

The fourth call. She cut the call. And then my phone beeped. It was a text from Shaina. I read the text. Once aloud, and once in my head, just to make sure ...

Reach AIIMS hospital as soon as possible.

My heart beat faster than it already was, but I was scared now. I took a few deep breaths and leaned against the door. Hospital?

On my way to the hospital I wondered if Dad had got Manoj beaten up, and that was why they had called me. But he wouldn't do that without asking me. Even if he did get Manoj beaten up, I didn't feel sorry for him.

I checked for a familiar name or a surname in the admissions register. The nurse noticed me losing it, and helped me out; she checked the registers herself and told me Ms Gupta was admitted in the ICU. It wasn't Manoj who was hurt.

Shaina Gupta? Diya Gupta? Or their mom?

I walked briskly towards the stairs, struggling to stay in control. The corridors were crowded with people and doctors ambling around. A few men were sleeping on the floor, some waited outside closed doors, crying and sobbing. I tried to think the best I could. Once I reached the second floor, I ran uncontrollably towards the operation theatre. I spotted Shaina in a bright red sari, her face buried in her palms, crying softly; I was relieved to see she was all right. I looked for Diya and her mom but couldn't find either one of them.

'What happened?' I asked as I went up to Shaina. I resisted an urge to hug her. Seeing her cry was just wrong.

'Diya . . .' she said. Her voice trailed off. I saw other people standing at a distance. A woman was crying uncontrollably in a corner with two women who tried to console her while they cried too. A couple of men were talking animatedly in the corner.

'What happened to her?' I asked. Before she could answer I saw Manoj walk towards me—big strides and anger writ on his face. 'Benoy,' I said. I shook his hand. His expression did not change. He hugged Shaina, who disappeared into his arms.

'What happened?' I asked.

He looked at Shaina, took her away and made her sit on one of the steel benches. He came back to where I was standing. I already did not like him. His eyes were vacant and there was something inherently evil in him.

'She had an accident,' he said. 'She was coming home in a rickshaw and a truck knocked it over. The rickshaw puller died on the spot. She's out of danger now and though she will live, the doctors have asked for another forty-eight hours.'

'Has she regained consciousness?' I asked.

'Once,' he answered.

'Why the fuck didn't you call me earlier?' I said, furious.

'You have no business here, Benoy. The doctors are taking care of her,' he said, staring me down.

'Go to hell,' I said and walked away to call Dad. His phone was unreachable and I dropped in a text explaining the turn of events.

I waited outside the door, with the crying, lamenting women and the two of them—Shaina and Manoj. I did not want to punch Manoj in his face and exacerbate their woes. *I have caused all this*. Diya was not supposed to attend the Career Launcher class that day. Had she not come for the class, she would have never taken the rickshaw. *I am responsible*.

Dad called me back and within an hour he was there. Walking beside him was the director and a senior doctor at AIIMS, Dr Juneja. My father introduced the doctor to an elderly man, Shaina's dad, and the doctor assured him everything would be okay.

'Mr Gupta, don't worry,' Dr Juneja said to Shaina's dad.

They were joined by Mrs Gupta. She was still crying and covered her mouth with her pallu to drown out the cries.

'Bhaisahib, you can do anything ... please save my child, please save my child,' she cried.

'Don't worry, behen, very experienced doctors are taking care of Diya. I am sure things will be fine. He's the director and he will personally take care of this case,' Dad said.

A few more doctors joined in the conversation. They said a few things in medical jargon, and then they left. Mr Gupta hugged Dad and thanked him profusely. Dad asked Manoj and me to leave, took Diya's parents into a corner and reassured them. I saw Diya's dad cry out suddenly and almost fall at my father's feet. Dad kept him from doing so and hugged him again. I found her parents sweet. They hardly looked or acted the way I had heard they did.

It had been three hours and she was still inside the operation theatre. The doctors working inside kept sending updates. *She will live. Things are getting better.* Every time they had good news to give us, we used to hug each other, and her parents thanked Dad. He kept saying he had done nothing, and it was the doctors who deserved the real credit, which was true.

Finally, the door flung open and the three doctors in green overalls came out rubbing their hands and talking to each other. All of us crowded the three of them and bombarded them with questions.

'She is safe,' the oldest doctor said. 'Can we talk to the parents of the patient, please? Alone?'

Diya's parents held each other's hands and followed the doctor. Diya's dad asked my father to come too. My dad followed them as they disappeared inside the doctor's chambers. The other relatives hugged each other in joy and relief. We all stood there and waited. Shaina was with her relatives, trying to console the aunts.

'Benoy?' Manoj said.

'Yes?' I said.

'I think you should leave now,' he said. 'And so should your father. Don't you see what *you* have done, Benoy? She was with *you* yesterday. She was supposed to be with her sister. Not you! *You* are responsible for all this. Get it?'

'But—'

'What will you get after ruining this family? First Shaina? Now this? Why don't you just go away? Nobody needs you here.'

'I was just trying to help.'

'We don't need your help! Shaina hates you for doing this to her sister. Just GET LOST,' he almost shouted and walked away.

Shaina hates me? She thinks I am responsible. Maybe she is right.

Though what Manoj had said was unpleasant, I was more worried about the conversation inside the doctor's chambers. I was too scared for Diya at that point to think about anything else. I *wanted* to see her. I still thought it was just a rude dream and I would wake up soon.

We waited outside the room and tried to overhear the conversation but we could not. We peered inside through the stained glass but we could not make out much from that either, so we just waited and fidgeted. I tried not to look at Manoj, who constantly stared me down. *You are responsible. Get lost.*

After a long time, they came out. My dad had his arms around her dad and her mother looked totally lost as she staggered out of the room. We all said our little prayers. Mrs Gupta fainted on one of the women and everybody rushed forward to pick her up. I was sick with worry now.

I went up to Dad, my hands trembling and my ears ready to hear the worst.

'What did he say?'

'She is fine. But, she cannot walk right now. She's paralysed waist down.'

What! I felt sick in the pit of the stomach and could have puked. Images of Diya bedridden and in a wheelchair flashed in front of my eyes. I felt her pain and it felt so wrong.

'What?' I asked, 'When will she be all right?'

'They are not saying anything.'

'What do you mean they are not saying anything? They must have given some *time frame*?'

'Benoy, they can't tell. She may walk some day, she may not. Nothing is *certain*.'

'What do you mean nothing is certain? Can't you do something about it? Better hospital? Better doctors?' I begged and blinked away my tears.

'We are looking at that,' Dad said.

Fuck. I am responsible. Every time this thought went through my head, I felt everyone looking at me and saying, '*You are responsible. Go away.*'

Diya's dad walked up to us and motioned that he wanted to talk to my father. Dad sent me away. I saw her dad folding his hands and my dad preventing him from doing that. They hugged each other for long and separated when Manoj went and told Mr Gupta that they could now meet Diya. Her parents and Shaina went inside the room that she was shifted into. They did not take long inside, hardly ten-odd minutes, and they came out. Her mother was still crying profusely and so was Shaina.

I asked Shaina about Diya and she shook her head. As I waited amongst those crying people, I felt bad to have caused pain to so many people. They did not need me. I had only brought in pain for both the sisters. I could not see them like this.

I have to go out of their lives.

Chapter Thirty-four

It had been quite some time that we had been waiting. It was three hours past noon. Manoj's family had gone back to their home. Manoj stayed back and his stares kept getting nastier. A few more relatives dropped in, talked to Diya's parents and left. We sat there motionless, waiting for the time that we could next talk to her. I desperately wanted to go inside and tell her that no matter what, I would always be there. But then, family comes first. I was just an outsider. *They did not need me.*

All this while, Dad had been making frantic calls everywhere and people/doctors had been coming in and out of the office of the doctors who operated on Diya. Nothing much came out of these conversations, except that the operation was carried out in the best way possible. There were talks about shifting her to another hospital, but they decided it was too early and right then she was too weak for that.

Although visitors are not allowed to stay on in the hospital, my dad pulled some strings so all of us could be with Diya. Over the night, the nurses came and went as we all stayed awake. Her parents and Shaina periodically went to meet her. I wanted to go and talk to Shaina about Diya, but Manoj never let her out of his sight. The nurses told me Diya was in her senses but in a lot of pain. She had to be kept on a constant dose of painkillers and morphine. The corridors were quiet in the night; I had heard Diya shouting from inside.

Loud cries. Curses. And sobs.

Maybe she had now been told about the unmoving legs. As I sat there, I was horrified to even think about what she must be going through. One moment she was in a rickshaw, looking forward to her sister's function, and the other moment, she lay in a bed, her legs motionless and with only a slight chance of recovery. She had her whole life in front of her. I shuddered. All the times that she had mentioned her LSE dreams came flashing in front of my eyes. Diya used to talk about them with so much fervour. She had such big dreams.

I closed my eyes and my first teardrops hit the floor. I hoped that when I opened my eyes, it would all be a dream and I would wake up in my bed. And everything would be the way it was. I sat alone on the steel bench thinking of what lay ahead of us. I needed someone to talk to, but that someone was on the bed, staring at a crippled life in front of her.

And it's because of me.

Chapter Thirty-five

It had been three days since Dad and I were there. They had begged us to leave, but I was not going anywhere until I saw her with my own eyes. And Dad just did not want to leave me alone. He had won me over in those three days. He was the person who took care of everyone. Dad made sure everyone ate on time and every time anybody needed a shoulder or a blanket, he was right there. Everyone slept at one point or the other, but he did not. He did all the running around, and took care of all the paperwork. He made sure that no one disturbed her parents.

'Uncle, you should leave now,' Shaina had said this at least a million times now, but Dad just lightly smiled and brushed aside the issue.

'Milk, beta? It's already late evening and you ate so little in the afternoon.'

'No, Uncle, I am good. Why don't you go back home and rest awhile? I am here. I will handle everything.'

'I don't need rest, beta. I will just get you some juice,' he said, ruffled her hair and left.

Shaina looked angrily at me.

'He is not going because you are still here. Why don't the two of you go back home and rest a little, Benoy? You haven't even slept in two days. You will fall sick, Benoy.'

'I will not.'

'Humph. Like father, like son,' she said and walked away.

Over the last few days, I had prayed day in, day out, for Diya's health and her recovery. It made me sick to think about what happened to her. No matter how much time passed, I could not come to terms with it. Shaina and I had hardly talked during those three days. Manoj had been there for more than a day and a half and never let her anywhere near me. Finally, his parents dragged him home.

It was the fourth night and I hadn't seen Diya yet. The horror and the pain of what Diya must have gone through had not lessened in my mind. Finally, Dad had dozed off in a chair. His mouth was wide open and his legs were on the chair in front of him. Shaina was still awake, but was sitting four or five benches away, occasionally tapping on her cell phone and sometimes just looking blankly through the wide-open spaces. She had been incredibly strong all this while. She did not cry much, took care of people around and encouraged everybody.

It was three in the night when I saw the nurse walking into Diya's room. I waited for her to come out and walked up to her. Shaina joined in too.

'Can we see her?' I asked the nurse.

The nurse motioned that she had just given her the medicine and that we should not take more than five minutes. She left. I looked at Shaina and asked if I should go in. She nodded, held my hand and we went in.

Wrapped in bandages and tucked inside a white blanket, Diya looked tired, her face was swollen and there were needles sticking into her skin. She looked drowsy. The monitors beeped. She could hardly react when she saw us. Shaina kissed her on the cheek. Diya smiled and she looked at me. We sat on both sides of her bed and smiled at her. I hoped she would feel better with us around. We didn't say anything.

'It would have been better had I died,' she said.

'Don't say that,' Shaina said.

'I am a cripple. I will always be that way. I should have died.'

Tears streamed down both their cheeks.

'You will always be our Diya. You are bigger than this. And we want you around. Ever thought what we would be without you?' Shaina asked.

'I just want to die.'

She did not stop crying, just looked at Shaina and me with tears in her eyes. Her eyes begged us to take her out of the pain of living the rest of her life confined to a wheelchair. It just sucked.

'You will be fine,' Shaina said.

Diya started to doze off. We settled her head on the pillow and left the room. Shaina was in tears again. We walked wordlessly towards the pharmacy to get ourselves a water bottle. Shaina started sobbing loudly and clutched me. She staggered and her legs gave way. I thought she would faint. I helped her up. We stood in the middle of the hallway and she kept crying. Her howls were loud. She bit me a few times, and dug her nails into me as she tried not to shout.

I don't know how much time passed. She just kept on crying. Every few minutes she used to lose her ground and fall over me. A little while later, we sat on a bench and she kept crying and hugging me. She kept repeating the same thing—*that she loved her and how she wished it had happened to her and not Diya*. I just hugged her and told her that things would be fine. I wished I could make it better for her.

'You know what?' She looked at me. 'I used to be so jealous of her. That she was so smart. And ambitious. I always used to feel bad about it and then taunt her on her clothes and her spectacles.'

'Hmm.'

'I never used to mean it. Never. She was always the most beautiful sister anyone could ever have,' she said and broke down again. As she cried, between her sobs, she kept telling me how much she loved her.

She drifted off to sleep and when she woke up, she realized that she was sleeping on my shoulder. She stood up with a start and smiled at me sheepishly. There were still tear marks on her cheeks. Her kajal was completely rubbed off and her naked eyes still looked as beautiful. From the corner of my eye, I saw Manoj and his older brother sitting on another bench. Shaina noticed it too. She looked at me.

'He is here,' she said.

'Yes, it's okay. Go.' I smiled.

As she started to leave, she said, 'Thank you, Benoy. I needed this. I needed to cry.'

'It's the least I can do. I'm sorry,' I said. 'Had she . . . not come to meet me—'

'Shut up, Benoy. *Never* think of that. Never,' she said and touched my arm.

Then she walked away. She sounded genuine. Maybe it was just Manoj who blamed me. Manoj hugged her again and looked at me. Probably to send me a message—*Shaina is mine.*

I was sitting on the bench, fiddling with my phone when for the first time in those days, Mrs Gupta came up to me. She was an elegant woman, but the last few days had been hard on her. She was in a terrible state and hardly looked like the two sisters had described her to me. She was sweet.

'Beta.'

'*Arre*, Aunty. Sit.'

She sat down next to me and said, 'Beta, you should go home now.'

'No, Aunty, it's okay. I can be a little help around here.'

'You have already done a lot, beta. You need some rest,' she said and ran her fingers through my hair. It reminded me of my mom.

'Aunty, you need rest. I am young and can handle this.'

She did not say anything for a while. I could see that she was trying too hard not to cry.

'Beta? Will you forgive us for that day? I cannot say anything to bhaisahib. I am too ashamed.'

'Not your fault, Aunty. Shaina must have felt that.'

'I don't know, beta. But you're a nice boy,' she said and got up. I could sense she was about to cry again. Her eyes were starting to tear up.

It was mid-afternoon when a doctor, who had flown in from Mumbai at my father's request, called Shaina, her parents and Dad to the chambers. As they moved in, Mrs Gupta looked at me and asked me to join too. I looked around and followed them. I could see Manoj standing in the corner, fidgeting in his place. He was furious at being left out.

'What is the news, doctor?' Dad asked the doctor as he looked through reports and results from various tests.

'Umm. The good news is that she doesn't suffer from paraplegia. Given the type of accident, she is very lucky.'

All of us looked at him with wide eyes, because we did not know what paraplegia meant.

'In paraplegia the patient loses all sensation in his or her legs, often up to the chest area . . . so that is not the case.'

He continued, 'See, when there is an injury to the spinal cord, it is usually incurable. What is done in the first thirty minutes of the trauma is what decides the fate of the patient. In this case, satisfactory care had been taken so she was saved from paraplegia. But since the injury was still significant, there was sufficient damage to the spinal area. So right now she suffers from partial paralysis.'

'Partial paralysis?' I asked.

'It is usually to one side of the body, but Diya has been lucky that her loss in movement is limited to her left leg. Though there is some loss on the right side too, but with the right treatment it will be okay. Even her left arm is fine only that she might have some trouble coordinating with that hand. With the right therapies she might get cured.'

'*Might?*' Diya's father asked.

'Sir, since the spinal cord cells don't have the ability to regenerate or repair, often such damage is permanent.'

'So you mean there is a chance she may never walk again?' Mr Gupta said.

'There is always the worst-case scenario. But, there is a very strong chance that she can improve and with the right therapies she should be able to do most of the things that a normal person can do,' he said.

Most things that a normal person can do.

People around me broke down into tears, hugged each other and talked about gods and godfathers they could go to in order to get her cured. I was a little relieved though. Earlier we had been told that she would never be able to walk again or even do the very basic things. That she would be trapped in a wheelchair. But to hear that she would be able to walk, even if with a crutch, gave me huge strength. Moreover, he said that with the right therapies she might be almost fully cured too. She might even walk like she *used* to.

The aunties and her mother kept asking the doctors

questions about the therapies and how long it would take her to walk again. The doctor gave vague answers to every question of theirs and I did not blame him for that. The meeting went on for over an hour after which everyone was just sadder. Everyone was waiting for a miracle. I was happy with whatever we got.

Dad, Diya's father and I hung back and asked if he knew some hospital that she could be shifted to for the requisite therapy. He advised us to stay put at this hospital for the next week or so. He said that once the initial recovery was complete, she could be shifted to Escorts. Dad asked if she could be flown outside the country . . . anywhere, that might increase her chances of being cured. The doctor shook his head. Dad reiterated that money was not an issue. The doctor still advised against it.

Finally, after a lot of probing, he suggested two doctors in California who were partial-paralysis recovery experts. He asked Dad to talk to them and see if he could get them to fly down to Delhi or fly Diya out after she got a little better.

'Bhaisahib,' Dad said to her father, 'don't worry, I will get the two of them to India. We will get Diya to walk again.'

'But—'

'Don't worry about the money. She is our daughter too. Just pray that our beti walks again.'

I knew Dad had money. And I knew Diya's treatment would hardly dent his income. But spending hours in the hospital, spending entire days talking to doctors . . . it was a different thing altogether. These were the same people who had called him a bad father.

Later that day, Diya had woken up and all the aunties had gone in to see her. I wondered what happened inside. Also, Eshaan came to the hospital. He had gone to Vaishno Devi for five days and his phone was not working. I told him all that had happened in the last few days. He was distraught and shocked. Finally, after everyone had had his or her share of time with Diya, Eshaan and I got in. Every one of us had been instructed not to cry or say anything negative in front of her.

'I heard your dad is doing a lot,' Diya said as she looked at me. 'I heard doctors are coming in from California. Your dad is bringing them?'

'Umm.'

'Nothing will help,' she said.

She moved her left hand, and it just moved haphazardly; the tubes and the needles strained as she moved her hand around.

'I can't live with this.'

'Diya, the doctors are positive about your recovery. You should be too. Your arm will be perfectly fine after therapy. He said that—'

'Will I be able to walk?'

'See, I didn't go to the gym every day for nothing! Until the time that your left leg is cured, I will be your crutch! That's not too bad is it?' I said.

'Hmm. What do you think?' She looked at Eshaan.

'You will be fine. Just be positive. I just read on the

Internet that willpower is everything. That's what decides the rate of recovery more than anything else,' he said.

'That's what decides? Benoy, then you should ask those doctors to cancel their flights. I just need willpower, nothing else!' she mocked. Her will to live was questionable and I understood that. We left after the nurse came in and gave her medicine.

'Talked to her?' Shaina asked as I came out. I introduced Eshaan to Shaina and he left. 'What did she say?'

'She is sad. It's hard for her.'

'I know. She has lost the will to fight,' she said.

'Don't worry, we will make her want to fight. I am with you, Shaina.'

'I am sorry for earlier, Benoy. And I am sorry for my parents,' she murmured.

'It's okay. You don't have to be sorry for anything to me! Ever,' I said.

'I just want you to understand that Manoj wanted me to stay away from you. And my parents. Maybe this is God's way of punishing me for what I did to you.'

'God doesn't punish cute people like you.'

'Manoj hates you,' she said. 'Even more now.'

Before I could say anything, Manoj reappeared, probably from hell, in the corridor and she had to go. Manoj gave me his badass look, to which I was immune.

The day before, Diya's mom had come up to me and said, 'You shouldn't take the blame on yourself. It's God's wish. If someone says something, don't mind.'

I was pretty sure Manoj had tried influencing her too.

However, I had started to feel that her parents liked me and my father. They had realized that they had committed a mistake in judging us. Probably, they were still angry with their daughter for she had broken their trust, but they were okay with us.

My dad's a stud after all.

Chapter Thirty-six

It had been more than a month since Diya had been in that terrible accident. All the relatives had disappeared after the initial concern. My days had a very specific schedule. I had to pick Diya up from her place every morning, take her to Escorts for her therapy, go to college and make notes of every single class that I attended. Diya had been very strict about this. She did not want to miss anything that happened in college. So consequently, I had to sit on the first seat and write down everything that was taught in class.

After classes, I had to go back to the hospital, pick her up and drop her at her place. Often, I used to end up having dinner at her place. Sometimes, Dad, too, dropped in. Over the last month or so, they had become like an extended family to us. Her parents had begun to love me. But then again, I owed it to Diya. My life had been totally empty before she walked in.

It was strange that they were the same parents we were all so scared about! But then, seeing your daughter almost die is a life-changing experience. And I guess who stays by your side during those times matters a lot.

When Diya had left hospital, it was hard for her to walk without someone accompanying her. Slowly, her condition had improved but she still used a walking stick. The one with four pegs at the bottom. Her left hand though was now totally functional. However, the bad news was that her progress had slowed down. The doctors were still putting in their best, but they were not positive about full recovery.

Her LSE dream was crushed though. Her treatment had already cost her parents a lot. Despite my dad's protests, her parents had paid for a part of her treatment. They paid whatever they could afford. It was not a lot, but it was a lot for them. However, she was not going to LSE any more, which was for sure.

~

'Beta,' Mrs Gupta said. I was in the kitchen helping her out.

'Yes, Aunty?'

'I think Manoj is coming over to see Diya.'

Shaina was still with him. I saw less of him now, though. We took care that I was not around when he was. It was apparent to everyone that we did not like each other.

'Oh, is he? I should leave then.'

'Oh, you don't have to, beta.'

'Aunty, you know that he doesn't like me around.'

'I know. I wish . . . I feel so bad sending you away every time he comes.'

'It's okay, Aunty. I know you will miss me, but I will come tomorrow again!' I joked.

'You are too nice, Benoy.'

'Aunty, I like your food. That's why I come here. It reminds me of Mom. So, I have an ulterior motive.'

'Who says I am not your mother? Don't I call you beta?'

'That's sweet, Aunty. Chalo, I will go now. Your *other son* must be reaching.'

'Yes, and take this. I have packed food for you.'

'For me? And Dad?'

'Ohh . . . I didn't pack for *bhaisahib*,' she said, already feeling guilty.

'Kidding, Aunty. See you tomorrow,' I said and left.

I knew that Aunty liked me more than she liked Manoj. But that was not enough. I wished it was the same for Shaina, too. Manoj had been doing everything to cut me off from the family. He even hired a taxi service for Diya, but it did not work because the taxi driver took many days off and she could not have afforded to miss a single day. Dad had bought me a Land Cruiser to facilitate the process, but Diya gave me hell every day for it.

'I didn't ask him to buy the car!' I said. 'He called you and told you that, right?'

'Yes, he did! But he will do whatever you would ask him to do. And I can walk now. It's not that I am totally incapable. Your big car makes me feel like shit, Benoy.'

'Whatever, Diya. Can't you just enjoy the luxury for a bit?'

'Why don't you start walking with my crutch and see what a luxury that is!' she retorted.

'You're such a pain in the ass! Differently abled my foot,' I said. 'Your ability is just to piss me off.'

'But I am sorry, Benoy, for being such a burden on you and your father. Like seriously.'

'Ohh, c'mon! Now don't start again! Dad and I have too much money or time. If I didn't have to carry you around, I don't know what I would do in life. I would probably kill myself in boredom,' I said.

'But I am sorry. You absolutely have no social life because of me. You must curse me for being a cripple.'

'Diya? Firstly, you are not a cripple. You will be fine! And secondly, *you* are my social life! You are my best friend and you are more than I will ever ask for.'

'But—'

'No buts. Just shut up.'

She started weeping.

'Now what? I can't deal with your PMS, man,' I complained.

'Shut up, Benoy. You wouldn't understand what I am making my family go through. They are so worried about who they will get me married to. You know the kind of people around me.'

'Oh, c'mon. Anyone would marry you! Okay, if you don't find anybody, I will marry you. Deal,' I said.

'I think that's what even Manoj's parents are waiting for,' she said sadly. 'My parents are so tense. They have been pushing all the functions back. Benoy, no one wants to get married to a girl who has a crippled sister. They are probably thinking they will have to take care of me after my parents are gone.'

'You are just imagining things, Diya.'

'He himself told Shaina so,' she said.

'Who? Manoj?'

'Yes. He hasn't told my dad in exact words but he has dropped hints. He keeps asking about my medical costs and my wedding . . . I am just twenty, Benoy; I can't take all this nonsense,' she said. 'Why can't they just leave me alone so that I can limp in silence?'

'You are thinking too much.'

'I'm not thinking too much. They haven't even come to our house even though they live just a few blocks down the street. What do you think?'

'I think it's great that your family has got rid of them. Has she asked Manoj about this?'

'No, what would she say? But she knows what they are up to.'

'Bastards.'

'I just want this to end. I hope I start walking without this fucking crutch,' she cursed.

'It's just a stick and you will be absolutely fine—I just hope so,' I said and parked the car in the compound and helped her get down from it. I smiled at the nurses and they took her away.

I couldn't wait for Manoj and his family to be dead and gone, away from Shaina, away from us.

Chapter Thirty-seven

Things were getting tougher for Diya. The medicines and the therapies were not working as well as they should have been. The doctors had almost given up hope, but Dad kept pushing them to work harder. That day I called Diya's mom to tell her that I had dropped Diya, but it was Shaina who answered. She was crying at the other end.

'Hi?'

'Hi, Benoy.'

'I just dropped her at the hospital. Why are you crying?' I asked. Silence. 'Are you crying, Shaina?' Silence. 'I need to see you right now. I'm coming over. Isn't your mom home?' Silence. I could only hear her cry. 'I will be there in twenty minutes.'

I rushed to her place and rang her bell incessantly till she opened it.

My God! Did she look beautiful! Sometimes, I thought that just her face was beautiful enough to spend one lifetime just looking at her. I let out a huge sigh and wondered how lucky Manoj must feel to have someone like her. Not for an hour or for a day, but *forever*. She looked beautiful as she smiled at me. Pretty beyond words, beyond poems, beyond epics.

'Everything okay?'

'Yes . . . umm . . . no,' she answered. Her voice became even sweeter as she got sad.

'What happened?'

She looked away. She had tears in her eyes.

'You are crying? Why? Look at me,' I said and instinctively went and sat closer to her, and took her hand into mine. I did not care if she was Manoj's or whoever's; I could not see her cry.

'Nothing.'

'Look at me and don't cry. You can tell me, and I am sure everything will be all right. Shaina? Don't cry, please. It feels so wrong when you cry.'

'It's just that . . . Manoj.'

'Manoj? What did he do? TELL me.'

'He just keeps making me feel bad about my sister, telling me that she's a cripple and that she won't ever walk again,' she said.

'Tell him she will be all right!' I grumbled. I hated it when people did not have confidence in her.

'He says he wouldn't be able to marry me until my sister is cured,' she said.

'What?' *That asshole.*

'Earlier, he used to give all kinds of excuses and I never said anything to him. But yesterday, I pushed him and he said very clearly that his parents wouldn't allow him to marry me.'

'*Fuck him!* How can he say that? And what if Diya, heaven forbid—?'

'His family wasn't very happy with his decision to marry me in the first place. They are in a huge debt. They wanted a hefty dowry, and Manoj's wedding was their last hope. Now they say all sorts of stuff to my parents and my parents can't say anything. I feel so stuck and responsible for all of this,' she said, holding her head in her palms.

'You are saying he won't marry you now because your parents cannot pay the dowry any more?'

'I don't know, Benoy. His parents have started looking for someone else for him.'

'And he doesn't say anything?' I asked, shocked. 'Can't you see, Shaina? He *doesn't* love you, Shaina. How can you *not* see that?'

She broke down. I held her hand again and tried to find words to soothe her, but I was too disgusted to say anything. At Manoj's parents, at Manoj and at Shaina. I just wanted to go to Manoj's place and knock his brains out.

'Everything will be okay. I will talk to Manoj.' I don't know why I said that.

'Please don't. He hates you and if he gets to know that I talk to you, he will beat . . . I mean, get very angry with me.'

'Does he *abuse you*?' I asked angrily.

'No! *Never*,' she said, rather unconvincingly.

'You can tell me that, if he ever—'

'No, he doesn't!' she suddenly shouted.

'Okay, fine,' I said. 'Calm down. So, what do you want me to do?'

'Nothing. I just wanted to tell somebody. I couldn't think of anyone but you.'

'I am glad that you thought about me.'

'I do, Benoy. I'm so sorry for whatever happened.'

'You look matchlessly beautiful even when you cry,' I said.

'I am with him, Benoy. When you talk like this, it just—'

'Just?'

'It messes with my mind.'

'Hmm.'

'You should go now,' she said.

'I think I should,' I replied. I wouldn't see her for the next two weeks.

Chapter Thirty-eight

Another fortnight had passed by, and Diya was getting better. That day, Diya did not say anything while in the car. Since I was the only person she used to talk to, she had loads to talk about. Finally, I couldn't take the silence and asked her. I was a little afraid that it would be about her condition.

'What happened?'

'What? Nothing,' she said and looked out of the window.

'Why are you so quiet today? Is it the big car? Or is it the fact that you're disabled? What's troubling you?'

'I told you, it's nothing,' she said.

'It cannot be nothing. Tell me,' I insisted.

'Benoy, Manoj's parents are coming over tonight to decide on the engagement date and other details.'

'Tonight? Why didn't anyone tell me?' I asked, shocked.

'They just called this morning to confirm, and I just can't take it. I just HATE the guy.'

'And Shaina?'

'I know she's my sister, but she's being stupid. She's just so scared of this Manoj guy. She just can't seem to extricate herself from this relationship. It's so irritating. She's a different person with me and with you, but you leave her with him, she becomes his slave.'

'I don't know what to say to that,' I said.

'He is not right for her. You are.'

'Shaina doesn't think so, Diya. I met her and I tried to tell her what I felt, but she is not concerned. I think she likes me, but not enough to leave him for me,' I explained.

'I just want to see her happy. She is happiest when she is with you. You're so sweet and selfless. That's what she needs, not a controlling bastard.'

'But—'

'What but? See, Benoy. For Shaina, it's hard. Every relative of ours knows about Manoj. There is a lot of pressure on her.'

'So?'

'So she cannot back out of the relationship. It would be very humiliating for our family. People will call her a slut. Just think, Benoy. She would never do it, no matter how much she likes you,' she explained.

'So what do you suggest?'

'That you're a fool. You should go there and get what's yours. You're the richest idiot I have ever seen, Benoy. You drive around in ridiculous cars, you wear all these expensive clothes, you're sweet and you're charming, and you can't make a girl fall in love with you? How utterly nonsensical is that? It's ridiculous!'

'But you always said my clothes are ridiculous?'

'But they look good on you. Like, not runway-model good, but decent. Benoy, I don't want my sister to get married there. I don't want that guy anywhere near my sister. It's all up to you. Be the charming flirt we all thought you were!'

'I can't flirt!'

'With her, you don't have to,' she said.

'You might be disabled, but you're certainly getting smarter.'

Chapter Thirty-nine

I called up Shaina on my way back home, trying to be what people expected me to be like: flirtatious and charming, two words that I was sure I wasn't.

'Hi. Where are you?'

'I was just going to college,' she said.

'Can we meet for a little while? I just dropped your sister to the hospital, so I needed to talk to you,' I said.

'Oh. Is it something important?'

'Yes, it is,' I answered quietly. She told me she was near my old house and I asked her to stay there.

I drove like a madman.

~

'Hey,' she said. She seemed happy, and she was smiling. I wondered if Diya had made a big deal out of nothing.

'Hi. You seem happy!' I said. 'Hey, do you mind if we

hang out at my place? I promise I will not do anything this time. It's too hot out here.'

She nodded. We walked to my house and I let her in.

'You said there was something important you wanted to tell me about Diya. What was it?' she asked.

'When did I say that?'

'You did! You said you just dropped her at the hospital and you wanted to talk to me about something important,' she repeated my words.

'I never said it was about her!' I said.

'You're so sneaky, Benoy,' she responded and laughed.

'I heard Manoj is coming tonight, and that you guys will decide on the engagement date. Are you excited?' I asked.

'Excited? I am not sure,' she said. 'And they were about to come tonight, but I think they are not. They are yet to let us know.'

'Does he trouble you any more?' I asked.

'I am used to it,' Shaina answered.

'The only things you should be used to are the good things people say about you. Do you want water? Let me get some,' I said and got her water from the fridge.

'Isn't that water old?' she asked.

'My maid still comes every day,' I said. 'This is as fresh as fresh can be.'

'Why do I forget you have secret stashes of gold biscuits hidden all over the country!' she mocked.

'You sound like your sister,' I pointed out. 'But unfortunately, I am not in love with your sister.'

'Stop it, Benoy,' she said shyly. 'You have to stop doing that.'

'Stop doing it? Are you crazy? You're like getting married tomorrow!'

'NOT TOMORROW!'

'Whatever. You're getting engaged in a month or so. I think I should make up for all the time to hit on you!' I said.

'Okay, fine. Enough.' She laughed. 'I should really go. If Manoj gets to know anything of this, he will probably kill me, and then kill you.'

'Ask him to try. I am a Delhi boy, man. Doesn't he know who my father is? He fucking owns half of Delhi.' I chuckled. 'And still you're with him. I don't see any reason why!'

'I should really go,' she said and smiled again.

'You should really stay. I am getting people to lock the door from outside. Not normal locks, but the titanium ones, ones you can't break into. We will be locked here forever.'

'Why do you say things like *that*?'

'Because I love you. And I will never say things like this to anyone else.'

'Why do you make my life so complicated? Things were better when you weren't around, Benoy,' she said.

'Because *I love you*.'

'If I were you, I would hate me with everything I have got. How are you so persistent? I have done everything wrong and still you won't go?' she said guiltily.

'I only fall more in love with you,' I answered.

'This is why I stay away from you,' she said.

'Why?'

'Because you are charming, and sweet.'

'But why stay away from me?' I asked and put my best smile on. 'You can just ask Manoj and his family to fuck off. That's all you need to do.'

'You know I can't do that,' she said. 'And now, I really need to go. The longer I stay, the more I would want to stay. I can't afford that. I can't mess it up again. I am very scared.'

'Why are you scared?'

'That I might fall for you,' she said and looked away. 'I have thought about the two of us together, and it's beautiful. But I feel terrible about it. *Guilty.*'

Her voice was heavy and serious. She looked even prettier now that she had told me that I was on her mind. Just knowing that I meant something to her meant the world to me.

'You don't have to feel guilty. I don't feel guilty about hitting on a girl who is about to get engaged.'

'Very funny, Benoy. It's different. You wouldn't understand.'

'I would. But the last time I wanted to understand you, you called me a spoilt brat and a stalker!'

She laughed. And she looked *oh so cute!*

'Brat you are. Sorry for the last part. Manoj wanted me to say that. Almost everything I said about you was just a repetition of his words, the things he wanted me to say. You know I would never say those things about you. I was so fond of you! I still am,' she clarified.

'It's okay. Obviously I know. So you don't regret anything that happened between us?'

'No. It was the best time ever!' she said and smiled at me.

'Not even the kiss?'

'Especially not the *kiss*,' she said, her eyes half open, half closed. 'It was my best kiss ever.'

'Hmm.'

She said this and came and sat close to me. Inches away. I did not know how to react. Her hand crept up mine, and I was scared. I didn't want to kiss her again and lose her. That would be just the worst.

'Maybe, it was not meant to be,' she said and looked deep into my eyes.

'It is . . . and err . . . I wish I was drunk.'

'Why?'

'Then I wouldn't be sorry for thinking about what I want to do to you,' I said.

I don't know why she came close to me. She must have come to make me feel better, but I was undergoing an entirely different set of emotions. Like the ones I had gone through that day when she was drenched and had got naked at my place.

'What do you want to do?' she asked, almost whispered with her lips slightly apart.

'I would rather not say. The last time I tried something, you left my place crying.'

'I think you should try whatever you want to,' she said, her hand rubbed against mine. This was getting creepy. Creepy but nice. *What the hell!* I decided to tell her what was on my mind.

'I would have kissed you. Kissed you and made you shut up about Manoj and the crap that is going to happen tonight. Wrap my lips around yours and kiss you long enough to make you realize that I am what you want, not him.'

'*Do it*,' I heard her say faintly.

'What?'

'*Do it*, Benoy.'

I made sure of what she said. And then . . . I leaned into her. Her eyes never let go of mine. Her hand clutched my hand tighter. Still centimetres away from her lips, my eyes closed as I could already sense the overwhelming pleasure. Time froze as my lips touched hers, the soft wetness of her soft, pink lips against mine, and our bodies met. I lost myself in the kiss, as my lips warmed up to her and I kissed her out of passion and not out of studied style. I did not know what I was doing. I had lost my senses. The kiss lasted for ten years, and my heart beat out of my chest. The wetness and the passion of the kiss had reached every iota of blood rushing through my body. As my eyes closed and opened periodically, I looked at her. And every time I saw her, I only kissed her more, my hands gripped her tighter, as if never to let go.

I was out of breath by the time I stopped kissing. I didn't want to stop.

'*I love you*,' I said.

'Don't spoil it,' she said and bent into me.

She looked at me with her eyes half drowsy and her lips wet from the kiss we'd shared. I felt her fingers on my neck and she let her nails linger there. Slowly, she moved down and her fingers hovered around the first button of my shirt. She still looked deep into my eyes. Then, she leaned further

·on to me and kissed my ear. Her tongue played with my ear while her fingers skilfully unbuttoned me. Her hands and fingers were all over me, teasing me and taunting me. Her eyes, her hands, her touch—everything drew me closer into her. It seemed like a dream. Her every touch, her every move owned me. I was hers.

'Take this off,' she whispered in my ear.

I got rid of my shirt. She pushed me on the couch and climbed on top of me. She kissed me on my lips again. I tried grabbing her, but she pushed away my hands. She started kissing me on my neck, licking it and biting it softly. She moved down, slowly kissing my chest and further down. Her eyes never left my gaze and I kept looking back at her. I felt helpless as she moved down and unbuckled my belt. The belt was snapped open.

'*What* do you want me to do?' she asked.

I was too numb to say anything, and she unhooked the button of my jeans. My feelings had no bounds, no explanations, everything turned hazy. And nice.

'Take it off,' she said again. But before I could, she did so. She looked at me and smiled. She sat up and removed her T-shirt. And then the *rest* of her clothes. She was right on top of me. *Bare.* I looked at her in disbelief. My body underwent a million internal orgasms as I saw her. The shapely hourglass figure wrapped in the most exquisite and perfect skin. The gorgeous breasts. The light coming from behind her accentuated her features and she looked *perfect*. Between that day when she had changed out of her clothes at my place and this day, I had imagined her naked quite a few times but this was better!

'You need help,' she said and looked at me. I felt her hand creeping down. My toes contorted as she weaved her magic around me.

'Was that good?' she said as she looked up at me.

Her eyes still dripped with unbridled passion and lust. I did not say anything. I just grabbed her. Her body was as smooth as porcelain, and it was phenomenal just to touch her. I could not help but dig into her. My tongue, my lips went all over her, as I flipped her over and went on top of her. She struggled a little but then gave in. My senses got clouded with her perfume and her touch, and I ravished her. I kissed and licked, almost to prove myself. She locked her legs around me and moaned. And every time she moaned it only made me savage her more. I sank my head into her gorgeous breasts and she kissed my forehead. And we suddenly started kissing again.

'We should do it,' I said.

'You think?'

'Yes,' I said.

'I thought you would never ask, Benoy,' she said and kissed me. Soon, I found myself again lying on my back. She climbed over me, and kissed me. What we did next would never leave my head. Our bodies collided and *we made love*. It did not matter when we rolled off the couch. It did not matter and we did not care when we were on the dining table. I have no idea how we reached the bedroom. But I do remember that I did not let go of her bare skin. My fingers never let go of her skin, her touch never left mine. We kissed until we ran out of breath. We bit and clawed our way into each other. Our hands were all over each other. So were we. We lost count of time and space.

Three hours later.

We lay next to each other, on the floor. I was exhausted and panting. She lay beside me. I looked at her and caught her looking at me. Her eyes had small tears that were streaking down. But she was smiling. I crept my hand up on the floor and she clutched it. She rolled over on to me and hugged me. It was not the fact that we'd made love that I was smiling about. What made me smile was that she looked at me with such love in her eyes. Maybe, I was imagining it, but it sure made my day. She slept with her head on my chest; she kissed me whenever she woke up. And I kissed her on the forehead whenever I got the chance. I did not know what she was thinking, but I knew what I was thinking.

Has this really happened?

Things suddenly changed in my head. This was an entirely new concept of Shaina in my head. She was a pretty and cute girl, who had been so guilty about briefly kissing me that day. But this was different. It was an entirely different side of her. And this side was incredibly seductive and sexy. As we snuggled and periodically kissed, we did not say anything. I did not know what to say. I don't know how much time passed. But my reverie was broken by her phone buzzing on the table.

'Ohh shit! It's seven,' she said; her phone kept ringing. It was her mom.

'Hi, Mom,' she said. 'Yes, Mom. With Benoy. Yes, I am just coming. Thirty minutes.'

She immediately got up and looked for her clothes. I

tried not to look at her as she changed. I got up, too, and got into my clothes.

'Need to go, Benoy. Manoj is home. They are home!'

'Ohh.'

'Shit! Why did I tell Mom I was with you!'

'Did your mom tell him?'

'I don't know,' she said. 'Can you drop me home?'

'Oh fuck! I had to pick up Diya from the hospital.'

'She's already home,' she said and checked her face in the mirror.

She was worried. And tense. I drove faster. I did not know what to say. Just a few minutes back, we were lying in each other's arms, naked, and now she was on her way to decide on which date she had to get engaged. I was furious, but my skin was still tingling from before.

Just as she got down from the car, I asked her, 'So?'

'So?'

'What about today?' I asked.

'Benoy?' she asked. 'Do you mind coming upstairs?'

'ME? Are you crazy? Your bastard boyfriend and his family is there,' I grumbled.

'Please,' she pleaded.

I couldn't say no.

Chapter Forty

M rs Gupta opened the door.
'Hey, beta! What took you so long?'

'Traffic,' I said, trying to compose myself.

'Shaina.' She turned to her daughter. 'Why don't you make him sit at the dining table? Call your sister, too. She's sleeping I think.'

We walked to the dining area and I couldn't see Manoj or his family there. Shaina's father was missing, too, so I assumed they had gone for a walk or something that adults do. 'Where is everybody?' I whispered in Shaina's ear.

'They must have gone out,' Shaina told me. Diya came out of her bedroom, rubbing her eyes, still sleepy.

'What are you doing here?' Diya asked as she saw me.

'Diya beta. You also sit down with them. I will serve all three of you together,' she said and Diya joined us at the table as well.

'Are you sure we should eat, Aunty? Shouldn't we wait

for Uncle and the others?' I asked but Mrs Gupta was too busy filling up the plates in front of us. She pointed out to the different casseroles in front of us and told me I shouldn't feel shy and I should eat whatever I felt like. She disappeared into her bedroom.

'You were sleeping inside?' I asked Diya. 'Didn't you meet Manoj and his family?'

Before Diya could answer, Shaina butted in, 'They don't like Diya. So Mom must have asked her to be in her room. Is that right, Diya?'

Diya smiled and nodded.

'It will be so strange if they walk in now and see us all eating,' I said.

'I don't care what that bastard thinks,' Diya said with disdain. 'Where were the two of you?' she asked us.

'We were hanging out at his place, but then Mom called and told me that Manoj and his family were here to decide the date of our engagement. So we rushed back!' Shaina explained.

'Aha! Okay,' Diya said and nodded her head. 'I'm surprised you're here, Benoy. Manoj hates you; you clearly love my sister. On a scale of one to ten, you're clearly a ten as far as undesirability goes.'

'She wanted me to be here,' I said, gulping as fast as I could. I wanted to run out before Manoj came, because I would have punched him otherwise. 'If left to me, I would thrash Manoj to inches away from his death, and then thrash him some more.'

'You would have done nothing!' Shaina argued.

'Excuse me?' I said.

'What excuse me? You just sit where you are and try to act all wise and understanding, Benoy. Why couldn't you just tell me that I should walk out of this wedding?' Shaina bellowed.

'I agree with my sister,' Diya said.

'Excuse me! The last time I said I loved you, you said I was spoiling it! And you were ALWAYS SO FUCKING HAPPY marrying this guy!'

'But I could have been happier with *you*. I know that. You know that. You didn't even have the balls to talk to my parents once about you and me. They love YOU! And you still couldn't tell them that you loved me,' Shaina argued.

'Yes, I agree again. You don't deserve her, Benoy,' Diya added.

'You know, FUCK BOTH OF YOU! I was the one who was crying day after day after day, and you, Shaina, were the one frolicking around with that bastard! And you blame me for this mess? When have I ever taken a step back from saying that I love you and that you're the best thing that ever happened to me?' I said and banged my fist on the table.

'You never fought for me, Benoy,' Shaina said and looked away.

'Totally,' Diya said, still eating.

'You know. GET LOST! Both of you,' I shouted and got up. 'I am fucking leaving. I am not into your games. *I love you but you never fought for me! I am with that guy but I have no problems kissing you and then dumping you for no good reason. He's an asshole but I will still be with him.* I'm DONE with all this!'

I started putting my shoes back on.

'See, you're still running,' Diya pointed out.

'You're always running,' Shaina said.

'Manoj and his family are minutes away from getting here,' Shaina said.

'And if you loved my sister as much as you say you do, you wouldn't be leaving. You would sit here, punch him in the face and kiss Shaina right in front of his family. Instead, you choose to run. You're a coward, Benoy,' Diya said, disgusted.

'FINE! I will just stay here and show that bastard his place. I will beat him up, right here, in front of his parents, and in front of yours. Don't give your community crap then! Don't go telling me that your parents would lose all their respect and their daughter is a slut. I am SERIOUS. I WILL FUCK THE GUY UP!' I growled and clenched my fist.

'We will see,' Diya said and Shaina nodded. They sat on the sofa while I paced around the room, trying to remain angry, reminding myself of everything I had faced because of Manoj.

Twenty minutes passed by.

'Where the fuck are they?' I asked angrily.

'Maybe they just knew you would beat them up, and hence decided not to come,' Diya said.

'I think that's a fair assumption,' Shaina said and laughed, and then Diya laughed.

'What the fuck is going on here?' I asked Shaina.

She got up from the sofa and walked up to me. She put her arms around me and kissed me on my cheek. 'No one's coming,' she said.

'What do you mean?' I asked, perplexed.

'I broke up with him two weeks ago,' Shaina said. 'The day I met you and cried. I had already broken up with him, but I thought I would go back. But then you called and came over, and I knew if I went back then, it would be the biggest mistake ever.'

'You knew?' I looked at Diya.

'Of course I knew!' she exclaimed.

'So Manoj's chapter is like finished? He's not coming? Like no engagement and all the bull crap?' I asked in disbelief.

Shaina kissed me again. 'Nope!'

'Why didn't you guys tell me? I was dying. I was literally dying!' I shouted.

'I wanted to tell you,' Shaina said. 'I wanted to run to you the moment I knew I had to be with you, but Diya wanted you to toil after me! Trust me, it was hard for me to stay away.'

I kissed her.

'You're a witch, Diya,' I said. 'You should know that!'

'If it weren't for me, you two wouldn't have met,' she countered.

'You never know,' Shaina said.

'I love you, Shaina,' I professed and turned to her.

'I love you more,' she said and kissed me on my lips.

'That's gross. This is officially the worst day of my life,' Diya said.

ALSO IN PENGUIN METRO READS

Till the Last Breath . . .

Durjoy Datta

When death is that close, will your heart skip a beat?

Two patients are admitted to room no. 509. One is a brilliant nineteen-year-old medical student, suffering from an incurable, fatal disease. She counts every extra breath as a blessing. The other is a twenty-five-year-old drug addict whose organs are slowly giving up. He can't wait to get rid of his body. To him, the sooner the better.

Two reputed doctors, fighting their own demons from the past, are trying everything to keep these two patients alive, even putting their medical licences at risk.

These last days in the hospital change the two patients, their doctors and all the other people around them in ways they had never imagined.

Till the Last Breath . . . is a deeply sensitive story which reminds us what it means to be alive.

If It's Not Forever
It's Not Love

Durjoy Datta • Nikita Singh

To the everlasting power of love . . .

When Deb, an author and publisher, survives the bomb blasts at Chandni Chowk, he knows his life is nothing short of a miracle. And though he escapes with minor injuries, he is haunted by the images and voices that he heard on that unfortunate day.

Even as he recovers, his feet take him to where the blasts took place. From the burnt remains he discovers a diary. It seems to belong to a dead man who was deeply in love with a girl. As he reads the heartbreaking narrative, he knows that this story must never be left incomplete. Thus begins Deb's journey with his girlfriend, Avantika, and his best friend, Shrey, to hand over the diary to the man's beloved.

Deeply engrossing and powerfully told, *If It's Not Forever . . .* tells an unforgettable tale of love and life.